The Gunsmith watched as the sore loser drew his gun, intending to kill the big winner.

"Don't do it," Clint cried out, but the man was beyond hearing. The Gunsmith drew and fired in one incredibly swift motion. The slug went into the man's left shoulder, knocking him down. With a look of shock on his face he aimed at the Gunsmith, who had no choice but to fire again, hitting the man in his chest.

"You saved my life," the man with the full house said.

The Gunsmith was about to reply when he heard a gun being cocked behind him.

"This here's the law speaking, friend, I saw you kill that man . . ."

Don't miss any of the lusty, hard-riding action in the new Charter Western series, THE GUNSMITH:

And coming next month:

Dedication

To Lobo Loren, The Decatur Kid, and Waco,
from The Brooklyn Kid

ONE

The Gunsmith did not often alter his style of dress, but San Francisco seemed to demand it.

He had been in the city for three days now, and still there was no sign of Jim West, whose summons he had come in answer to. All he'd had time to do was buy some new clothes, gamble and make the acquaintance of the beautiful Jacqueline, or Lady Jackie, as she preferred to be called.

They had met at the Bella Union, one of the many gambling houses in Portsmouth Square. Clint Adams enjoyed his poker, and enjoyed going up against the best players. In the West you didn't find many women who played poker at all let alone a "good game" of poker—but you'd find more than a few in San Francisco, since the city drew good gamblers just like honey draws flies.

They had been seated across the table from each other. Clint had noticed her immediately and was sure that the same had been true of her. Soon, however, the only thing they had each become interested in that first night was the other's ability to play poker. It was after the game that they became interested in other abilities.

That was Clint's first night in San Francisco, and had it not been for the Lady Jackie the next two days might have passed much more slowly and uninterestingly.

Clint's first image of the fourth day was the top of Lady

Jackie's head between his legs as she skillfully used her tongue to bring him awake—and erect.

"Jackie—"

She looked up at him with a lascivious smile and said, "Good morning, sleepyhead."

He could not quite get used to the wanton, uninhibited woman who lived in the body of the icy cool, sophisticated Lady Jacqueline Dulles. She was energetic and inventive and was a pleasant surprise to Clint the first time they went to bed together. After the poker game was over they had gone to Clint's room at the Alhambra, rather than hers at the Parker House, and there she had shed that veneer of sophistication as if it had come off along with her clothes.

Now she continued to work on his erection with her tongue, licking it up and down along its entire length, and then finally she captured the swollen head of it in her mouth and began to suck while her fingers worked its length.

"Jesus, Jackie—" Clint said, raising his hips up off the bed.

She laughed throatily without allowing him out of her mouth, and began to suck furiously, her head bobbing while her fist worked down and up.

"Jackie—" But then his legs began to tremble, his buttocks clenched, and suddenly he was spurting and she was swallowing . . .

After Lady Jackie had drifted off to sleep again, with her head on his shoulder, Clint started to worry about his friend Jim West. Here it was, the beginning of his fourth day in San Francisco, and still no word from the secret service agent. Clint had been in Labyrinth, Texas when he received the telegram from West asking him to go to San Francisco, register at the Alhambra, and wait to be contacted. That same day he mounted Duke, his big black gelding, and started out, leaving his team and gunsmithing rig behind. If Jim was asking for his help, it had to mean trouble, and Clint felt that the faster he got there, the better.

Now he had to wonder whether, in spite of his haste, he had arrived too late. Had something already happened to his friend?

The last time he'd heard from West he'd become involved with a lunatic trying to finance the rise of the New South with buried Confederate gold, and Clint had been called in by the President and the head of the secret service—Fenton—on West's recommendation.* Did President Grant and Fenton have anything to do with this summons to San Francisco? West and Clint were friends, but Jim had a tremendous loyalty to the service, and to the country, and would do whatever he had to do to protect them.

Clint's bad feeling about the entire matter doubled just as he heard someone outside his door. He slid out from beneath Lady Jackie, trying his best not to wake her, took his gun out of the holster that was hanging on the bedpost and started for the door. Immediately he noticed the envelope that had been slipped under it, but before bending down to pick it up he opened the door and as he'd expected found the hallway empty.

"What is it?" Lady Jackie asked, squinting sleepily from the bed. "What's wrong?"

"Nothing's wrong," he assured her. "I just got some mail."

"At this time of the morning?"

"I guess it's special delivery," he said.

He picked the envelope up off the floor and looked at it. There was nothing written on it but his name, and it was sealed. He went to tuck his gun into his waistband and then,

---

*The Gunsmith #10: New Orleans Fire

realizing that he was naked, padded back to the bedpost and replaced it in the holster. When he opened the envelope there was a sheet of paper with one line written on it: "Join me for breakfast downstairs."

"No signature," he said aloud, putting the paper back in the envelope.

"Hmm?" she asked without lifting her head from the pillow or opening her eyes.

Who else could the note be from? he thought. It had to be either West or Fenton because Ulysses S. Grant wasn't about to sit in the dining room of the Alhambra waiting for him.

He put his hands on his hips and looked down at the lovely form of Lady Jackie. The sheet was down to her waist, exposing the delicate curve of her back and the beginning of the slopes of her buttocks. He felt a stirring in his loins but knew he was going to have to put it off until later. Down in the dining room was the answer to why he had been called to San Francisco.

"Hmm?" Lady Jackie said again.

"It's nothing, my lady," he said. "I've just been invited to breakfast."

As he reached for his clothes Lady Jackie smiled without opening her eyes, licked her lips and said, "No, thank you, darling, I've had mine."

TWO

Clint dressed and reluctantly left Lady Jackie lying in bed alone, after giving the slopes of her buttocks a last, longing look.

When he got to the dining room he stopped just inside the entrance and scanned the room. He was looking for his friend, Jim West, but he was not surprised when he spotted West's boss, Fenton, seated at a corner table.

Fenton was a dapper man, tall and slim, about forty and—in the opinion of President Grant—somewhat delicate looking, which often made the bearish Grant feel uncomfortable. The man was good at his job, however, there was no denying that. Clint knew that West had a tremendous amount of respect for the man, but for some reason Clint didn't like him. As a matter of fact, West didn't like him either, but he did respect him.

Fenton stood up politely as Clint approached, but frowned as Clint said, by way of greeting, "You son of a bitch," and sat down.

"Perhaps I deserve that," Fenton said.

In order to assure Clint's help in the New Orleans business, Fenton had deceived him, and upon completion of the job, Clint had not returned to Washington to see either Fenton or President Grant.

"No *perhaps* about it, Fenton," Clint said. "I don't like the way you do your job."

"Be that as it may," Fenton said, "I get my job done, and so did you, in New Orleans."

"Not for you, though."

"Regardless of the reason, the President was very pleased," Fenton said. "He was also very disappointed that you didn't see fit to return to Washington. He was looking forward to meeting you."

"Sorry I disappointed him," Clint said, but his tone said that he was not sorry at all.

"All right," Fenton said. "I don't blame you for being bitter, but that's past. Let's put that behind us and get to the business at hand."

"I don't have any business with you, at hand or otherwise," Clint said.

"Now, don't be hasty, Adams," Fenton said. "Let me explain—"

"All I want you to explain to me is where Jim West is," Clint said. "Or did you simply send me a message with his name on it, without his knowledge?"

"No, no," Fenton said, "you have it wrong. I did send the message, but it was not without Jim's consent."

"You expect me to believe that?"

"If you'll let me explain from the beginning," Fenton said, "I don't think I will have any trouble convincing you."

Clint glowered at Fenton while he mulled it over, then relented, simply because he wanted to know what had happened to his friend.

"All right," Clint said. "Let me order some coffee, and then you can talk."

"Fine," Fenton said. "Uh, we'll just have the waiter put your order on my check."

"Well, thank you very much," Clint said.

When the waiter came over, Clint surprised Fenton by ordering not only coffee, but the largest, most expensive breakfast that the dining room had to offer.

"Anything for you?" Clint asked Fenton, who was frowning.

"Uh, no, just coffee," Fenton replied, and the waiter left.

"All right," Clint said, "go ahead and talk."

"I wouldn't have come to you if it wasn't important, Adams," Fenton began. "You must know that."

"Oh, I know that, all right," Clint assured the head of the secret service. "Whatever it is, you think it's of monumental importance—but I'll bet there are times when you feel that way about a haircut and a shave."

"I do not take my responsibilities to this country, or to General Grant, lightly," Fenton said tightly.

"Look, Fenton, we both know what a fire-breathing patriot you are. Can we get on with this?"

Fenton drew a deep breath and seethed silently, and when he did not respond to the Gunsmith's barb, Clint was sure that whatever was on the man's mind was indeed very important, to both him and the President.

"What we are talking about here," Fenton said, finally, "is General Grant's life."

"Has he been assassinated, then?" Clint asked. "I hadn't heard."

Again Fenton took a deep breath, and Clint decided that he'd stop trying to provoke the man and let him get on with his story.

"Two days ago, in Washington, D.C.," Fenton continued, "there was an attempt, and it came very close."

"What happened?"

"One of our agents was with the President at the time, and saved his life."

"What happened to the agent?"

"He was wounded. Took a bullet meant for General Grant. Even now we don't know if he'll live or die."

"What does all this have to do with me?" Clint asked. "The President is safe, isn't he? You've caught the would-be assassin."

"That's just it," Fenton said. "We haven't caught him, and we want him." Fenton leaned forward and added, "We want you to get him."

"Why me?"

"West seems to think you're the best man for the job," Fenton said. His tone indicated that he did not agree with his finest agent's assessment.

"And the President?"

"General Grant has a great deal of respect for West's opinion," Fenton said.

"I assume, then, that you know who this would-be assassin is?"

"Oh, he was identified, all right," Fenton said, "by West himself."

At that point Clint's breakfast was brought to the table and laid out before him, to Fenton's profound displeasure.

"Who is he, then?" Clint asked, when the waiter had finished setting it all out.

Fenton hesitated a moment, then said, "Paul Martel."

The name hit Clint right in his memory. Paul Martel, the self-styled general whose plan it was to lead the rise of the New South—a plan foiled by the Gunsmith!* After that, instead of killing Martel, Clint had let him go free. What could he do alone, he had thought, without his new army?

What, indeed?

"You can't turn this job down, Adams," Fenton said.

"Because of Martel?" Clint asked. "You think that's

---

*The Gunsmith #10: New Orleans Fire

enough of a reason for me to hunt a man down?''

"That's one reason," Fenton said. "You should have killed Martel when you had the chance. You left him alive, and he almost succeeded in killing General Grant—and he'll try again."

"If that's only one reason," Clint asked, ignoring the large repast that had been spread before him, "what's the other one?''

"The agent who was wounded," Fenton said, "and who may already be dead."

Clint felt a chill as he asked, "Who?"

"Jim West," Fenton replied.

THREE

Fenton waited patiently while the Gunsmith ate his breakfast, and Clint took his time eating it, so as to give himself sufficient time to think.

In truth, however, there wasn't all that much for Clint to think about. It was true that he had allowed a man to live—when he could have rightfully killed him—and the man had come back and had nearly killed the President of the United States. Clint would never have admitted it to Fenton, but he did feel a certain amount of responsibility for that. Then there was the matter of Jim West, who was one of Clint's closest friends, dead or damned near it because of Paul Martel.

"Where is Martel now?" Clint asked, leaning back from the table.

"One of our agents trailed him as far as the Alaskan border," Fenton answered.

"And no farther?"

"No farther," Fenton repeated. "His body was found last night. He'd been shot with the same gun that shot West."

"Then Martel could have crossed the border into Alaska, or doubled back."

"We assume he crossed into Alaska," Fenton said. "He'll want to put as much space between himself and us as possible, until he makes up his mind what he's going to do next."

"I guess I'll have to go by your assumptions," Clint said.

"It is our educated opinion," Fenton said stiffly, "that Martel crossed the border into Alaska. If you accept this assignment, you will act on that."

"Fine," Clint said, and Fenton showed some surprise that the Gunsmith did not argue the point.

"Again," Fenton went on, "if you accept the assignment, we will provide your transportation to the Alaskan border, much of which will be by private railroad car."

"And my horse."

Fenton frowned and said, "We can supply you with an excellent horse—"

"I want *my* horse," Clint said, cutting the other man off.

Fenton frowned again and asked, "Does this mean you're accepting the job?"

"As long as I get my horse."

"We'll transport your horse too," Fenton said. "Now I suppose you want to talk about some sort of recompense."

"No."

"No?" Fenton repeated, looking puzzled.

"No payment," Clint said. "All you have to do is pick up my expenses."

Clint wiped his mouth on a cloth napkin, dropped it on the table and stood up.

"Don't look so surprised, Fenton," Clint said, spreading his hands. "You've convinced me."

"Don't make me laugh, Adams. What is it you really want?"

"In payment?" Clint asked. "You're right, Fenton, I do want something."

"I knew it," Fenton said, looking smug. "What is it?"

"I want to see West," Clint said.

"What?" Fenton said. "Why?"

"Why?" Clint repeated. He leaned on the back of the chair

he had just vacated and said, "Because we both know that you're not above lying to me to get what you want, Fenton. I want to see West myself."

Fenton began tapping the fingers of his left hand on the table in annoyance. "You realize what a delay this will be?"

"If West was really shot—and accepting that he was, if it happened in Washington—then there will be a delay. That's tough."

Fenton's right hand joined his left hand in tapping on the table, and then he abruptly removed both hands from the table and said, "All right."

"All right what?" Clint asked.

"You can see him."

"In Washington?"

Fenton's lips pressed together until they almost turned white, and then he said, "No, here."

"The assassination attempt was here, in San Francisco?" Clint asked, incredulously.

"Yes," Fenton admitted, and it obviously hurt him to do so.

"How did you keep that quiet?"

"It wasn't easy," Fenton said. He stood up and asked, "When will you be able to travel?"

"Whenever your train is," Clint replied, "and after I see Jim."

"In the morning, then," Fenton said. "I will come by later tonight to take you to see your friend."

"That's generous of you."

Clint turned to leave, took a few steps, and then turned back, saying, "Oh, yes."

"What now?" Fenton asked. He himself was also about to leave the dining room.

Clint gestured toward the agitated waiter who was advancing towards them, waving a slip of paper, and said, "Don't forget to pay for the breakfast. It was delicious."

When the Gunsmith returned to his hotel room the Lady Jackie was awake but still naked in his bed. As he undressed to join her she stretched her splendid body luxuriously and kicked the sheet away so he could see every lovely inch of her.

"How was your breakfast?" she asked.

He joined her on the bed before answering.

"It was the best the hotel had to offer," he answered, taking her into his arms, "but somehow I don't think it was as enjoyable as yours."

Lady Jackie chuckled wickedly and moved down so that she could take his semi-hard cock into her mouth. It swelled quickly as she cupped his balls gently in one hand while she simultaneously pumped him with her other hand and sucked on him hungrily.

Although Clint had been distracted when he returned to the room, Lady Jackie's ministrations quickly occupied his attention. He cupped her head in his hands while she continued to suckle him furiously, and then he was flooding her mouth with a torrent of semen which she easily accommodated.

"I'm glad you came back so soon," she said, burying her face in his neck. "I was dying for seconds."

FOUR

R. T. Fenton angrily paid the breakfast check, and then quietly stalked out of the hotel, holding his temper in check as best he could. He had always thought that West—admittedly his finest agent—was the most infuriating man he'd ever met, with General Grant himself a close second, but now both of them had to move down on the list in deference to the Gunsmith, Clint Adams.

In front of the hotel Fenton hailed a cab and moved close to the driver so no one else would hear when he gave the man the address. He then got into the cab and, during the ride, made an effort to get himself back under the iron control he prided himself on. He would need all of the control he could muster while talking with the President. He was fiercely loyal to the President, but as a man Grant himself was another matter. He was crude, at best, and Fenton spent as little time in his company as possible. To his credit, he allowed the secret service director virtually to run his department as he saw fit, but from time to time, the man insisted on "keeping his hand in," as he put it—and Fenton could not fault him for that. Especially this time, after all, he was the one that Paul Martel had tried to kill.

In taking the bullets meant for the President, West had made Fenton's agency and Fenton himself look good in the process. Fenton could be grateful to West for that.

The nagging question in the back of Fenton's mind, however, was, How did Martel know that Grant would be in San Francisco? Grant's trip had basically been for pleasure, and had been very hush-hush. Grant's doctor had advised a few days rest, and Fenton had insisted that the President be accompanied by his best man.

There were two possible answers to his question. One: There was a leak in the President's staff, or in Fenton's; or two: It was a coincidence upon which Martel had immediately seized.

Fenton had already taken steps towards checking for staff leaks and then had left Washington with two of his men to assume the responsibility of protecting President Grant.

The driver pulled up at a house in a somewhat less than ostentatious section of the city; Fenton paid him, and then waited until he was out of sight before going inside.

In the foyer he found his first agent, on guard and alert, holding his gun ready until he recognized his superior.

"How is everything, Gordon?" Fenton asked.

"Quiet, sir. Very quiet."

"That's fine," Fenton said. "Where is the President?"

"He's in his room upstairs, sir."

"Fine," Fenton said again. "Carry on, Gordon."

"Yes, sir," the agent said, holstering his gun in his shoulder rig.

Fenton climbed the stairs to the second floor and found his other man exhibiting the same alertness.

"Good morning, sir," the man said.

"Good morning," Fenton said. "Is the President awake?"

"Yes, sir," the agent replied. "We just had his breakfast delivered. I brought it in to him."

"Very good, Martin," Fenton said. "I'll be in with the

President for a short while. One of you might want to go out and get something for both of you to eat."

"Yes, sir," Martin said. "Thank you, sir."

Fenton gave his man a short nod and said, "As long as one of you stays on duty in the foyer downstairs."

"Of course, sir."

Fenton knocked on the closed door and heard Grant's gruff voice tell him to come in.

"Good morning, sir," Fenton said, entering the room.

"Fenton," Grant said. He was seated at a small table that was covered with plates of eggs, potatoes, ham, biscuits and steak along with a bottle of whiskey. Fenton's stomach churned at the thought of washing down eggs with whiskey at that time of the day. "Damn, man, this isn't what my doctor had in mind when he recommended I relax, locking me up in one room."

"I realize that, sir," Fenton said, "but after the shooting, we dare not take any chances."

"We might as well go back to Washington, then," Grant said.

"I've thought of that, sir," Fenton said, "but when we do, we don't want anyone to know about it."

"Who's going to know?" Grant demanded.

"Who knew you were here in San Francisco, sir?" Fenton countered.

Grant made a face because he knew his secret service director was right, but that didn't mean he had to like it.

"Have a cup of coffee, Fenton," Grant said, pouring himself a whiskey, "or better yet, a drink."

"Coffee will do, sir," Fenton said. Why was the man constantly offering him whiskey when he knew he didn't drink?

"That's right, you don't drink, do you?"

"No, sir."

That was one of the things that bothered Grant about Fenton. The man did his job reasonably well, but there was just something in the President that would not allow him to completely trust a man who would not take a drink, not even to be sociable.

"How did your meeting with Clint Adams go?" Grant asked after Fenton had poured himself a cup of coffee.

"He has agreed to accept the assignment, on one condition," Fenton said.

"A condition?" Grant asked. "I thought you said you could handle the man, Fenton. He's making conditions now?"

"He'll go ahead with the assignment, sir," Fenton assured the President. "That's no problem."

"What's the condition?" Grant demanded.

"He wants to see West."

Grant frowned. "He's still alive, isn't he?"

"Yes, sir, he is—"

"Then let him see him, man!"

Fenton hesitated a moment before speaking, to make sure that his annoyance did not show in his tone of voice. "I am already taking steps to do that, sir. When I leave here I will arrange it with the hospital, and I will bring Adams over tonight. He will be ready to leave for Alaska tomorrow morning."

"Well, good," Grant said. "Maybe now I can get back to my breakfast."

Fenton was often surprised at what a buffoon Grant could appear to be because he knew what a sharp mind he really had. The buffoonery had to be an act, but if it was, it was so good that he found himself believing it half the time.

"Yes, sir," Fenton said, putting his cup down.

"I want you to report to me tonight, after you've taken

Adams to see West," Grant said. "I want to know West's condition. I owe my life to that young man."

"Yes, sir," Fenton said. "Would you like to see Adams, sir?"

"No," Grant said. "Not until he finishes what he started with Paul Martel. If he had killed the man when he had the chance, none of this would have happened."

"I believe he realizes that, sir," Fenton said.

"I hope so," Grant said.

Fenton turned to leave and Grant called him back.

"Fenton."

"Yes, sir."

The President hesitated, looking as if he had swallowed something that didn't agree with him, and then he said, "Good work."

"Thank you, sir."

Fenton left the room, feeling a fool for the rush of pride in himself he had felt when Grant complimented him. Still, even if he didn't like the President, he respected Grant for his leadership qualities, which had been proven time and again, so perhaps there was no harm in it.

When Fenton left the house, both of his agents noticed that their boss had a very satisfied look on his face.

FIVE

Clint Adams thought he had been cold when he was in Montana, along the Canadian border,* but Alaska was an entirely new experience for him. It didn't seem to bother Duke, though. The big black horse seemed to be weathering the cold quite well. Duke hadn't liked the boat ride any more than Clint himself had, and apparently the animal was just glad to get his feet—or hooves—on dry land, again.

Only, even that wasn't so dry. There was snow on the ground, and in some places it had thawed, forming puddles of water and mud.

"How the hell did I let us get talked into this one, big fella?" Clint asked aloud.

Duke simply shook his massive head, as if to say that he wasn't there when it happened, so he had no idea.

Back in San Francisco, Fenton had showed up in a cab to take Clint to see the injured West, and the Gunsmith had only been mildly surprised to find out that his friend actually had been hurt saving President Grant's life.

West was lying in bed, eyes closed, face very pale, with a nurse at his side.

"Satisfied?" Fenton asked.

"I'd like to talk to the doctor."

---

*The Gunsmith #12: The Canadian Payroll

A young doctor was brought in, and he explained that they had done everything they could for Mr. West. The rest was up to him.

"The man is in extraordinary physical condition, however," the doctor added. "I'd give him better than a fifty-fifty chance."

"Thank you, Doctor."

As the doctor left, Fenton once again asked Clint, "Are you satisfied?"

"Yes, all right," Clint said. "I'm satisfied."

"You'll be picked up in the morning and taken to the docks," Fenton said.

"The docks?" Clint asked. "I thought I was taking a train north."

"We decided to book you right on a steamship up the coast to Alaska."

"I've never been on a steamship," Clint said, sourly, but a last look at his friend told him it was a small price to pay.

He had second thoughts about that during the trip up the coast, but luckily the sea was calm and the Gunsmith got through the trip without too much discomfort. He didn't want to think about the trip home, except to wonder if it would be worth it to traverse the mountains that separated Alaska from the Yukon territory of Canada, just to avoid another steamship trip.

Alaska had only been a possession of the United States since 1867, when Secretary of State William H. Seward negotiated its purchase from Russia. Due to the vast stretches of unexplored land, the disagreeable climate and terrain, Alaska was then dubbed "Seward's Folly." Since then Alaska had been governed by military commanders from the war department, and it was a representative of that commander who met Clint at the docks.

"Mr. Adams?"

"That's right," Clint said, examining the man who approached him. He was tall and slim, with no meat on him; Clint had to wonder how he stood the cold. His face was pitted, and he had a small, brushlike mustache tucked under a large nose.

"My name is Mallerby, sir," the man said, extending his hand. "I am the assistant to the military commander, Captain Dale Walker. Welcome to Cordova."

Mallerby extended his hand and Clint took it in his right while holding Duke's reins with his left.

Mallerby looked past him and said, "Marvelous looking animal. Is he yours?"

"We're partners," Clint said.

"Yes," Mallerby said. "Marvelous. Well, shall we get your bags?"

"I've got everything right here," Clint said, indicating the saddlebags on Duke's back.

"Very well. I've taken the liberty of registering you at the hotel."

"Do you have any news on Martel?" Clint asked.

"I'm afraid we don't have a lot," Mallerby admitted, looking embarrassed. "Of course, the captain hoped to be here to meet you himself, but he was called away to the range area, just below Mount McKinley—"

"Could we get to the hotel, Mr. Mallerby?" Clint asked. "I could do with a wash."

"Certainly."

"After I freshen up, I'd like to get whatever information you have on Martel so I can get started after him."

"Of course. Follow me to the hotel."

Clint followed Mallerby down a street that was alternately hard and muddy.

"This is the main street," Mallerby said, making conversation.

"Doesn't look like much, does it?" Clint asked.

"Alaska is growing, Mr. Adams," Mallerby said, as if that explained everything.

Mallerby led Clint to a rundown, two story building that had a crudely drawn sign over the door that said HOTEL.

"Here we are."

"Fine," Clint said, turning away.

"Uh, where are you going?" the other man asked.

"Now that I know where the hotel is," Clint said, "I'd like to take care of my horse before I go in."

"May I bring your things in for you?" Mallerby asked.

"That's okay," Clint said. "I'll take care of them. Why don't you direct me to the nearest livery and then meet me back here in an hour?"

The man hesitated, then gave Clint directions, looking worried the whole time. Maybe he thought the military commander would think he wasn't doing his job right.

"See you in an hour," Clint told the younger man, and started for the livery with Duke in tow, shaking his head at what he'd gotten himself into.

SIX

After getting Duke settled in the livery Clint went back to the hotel, checked out his room, and then arranged with the clerk for a hot bath. The water had to be heated, and it cost plenty, but since the government was picking up his expenses, the Gunsmith didn't argue, he just enjoyed. He hadn't been able to bathe on board ship, and he could feel the layers of dirt he had built up over the past few days just sliding off of him.

When he got back to his room he still had some time left before Mallerby would show up to meet him, so he cleaned his weapons: the modified .45 Colt, the Springfield rifle, and the .22 New Line, which he was keeping tucked away in his saddlebags for now and which, once he was on Martel's trail, would be tucked into his belt inside his shirt.

He was putting the New Line away when there was a knock at the door. When he answered it he was holding his Colt, preparing to slide it into his holster, and Mallerby jumped a foot when he saw it.

"Oh, sorry," Clint said, holstering the weapon. "I was cleaning it."

"I see," Mallerby said, nervously. "I thought perhaps we'd have dinner together and discuss things."

"Fine," Clint said, "as long as you have the information I need. Let me get my hat."

25

Clint put on his hat, and then the heavy jacket he had bought when he was in Montana.

"Let's go," he said. "I hope this town has got a restaurant with some decent food."

"Nothing to match San Francisco, I'm afraid," Mallerby said, "but it's not bad."

Clint decided that if it "wasn't bad" Mallerby would have said something like "it's pretty good," and didn't hold out much hope for anything but a hot meal.

The café was in a rundown building, as in the case of the hotel, and there wasn't much to say about it as far as cleanliness went.

"The steak isn't bad," Mallerby said.

When the waitress—a woman in her mid-forties who didn't look too clean herself—came over, Clint said, "I think I'll just have a bowl of soup."

Mallerby thought a moment, then ordered the steak. Clint thought that it was for his benefit, so that he wouldn't think that Mallerby was trying to steer him wrong.

"I would have thought you would want a good meal," Mallerby said after the waitress left.

"In the morning," Clint said, and then added to himself, *What could they do to eggs?*

The waitress brought over a pot of coffee and two cups, and the Gunsmith immediately poured one for himself. He was not used to this kind of cold. He didn't even care what the coffee tasted like, as long as it was hot.

"I daresay this cold is something you are not used to," Mallerby said.

"You've got that right," Clint said, sipping the coffee again. It *wasn't* bad, after all. In fact, it was strong, the way he liked it.

"How is the coffee?" Mallerby asked.

"Not bad," Clint replied, shortly. Mallerby's eagerness to

please was starting to get to him. "Could we get down to business, Mr. Mallerby?"

"Call me John, please," the man replied.

"Fine," Clint said. "John, could we get down to it?"

"Of course," Mallerby said, pouring himself a cup of coffee. "There really isn't all that much to tell. By the time we got the message from Mr. Fulton, Paul Martel had already docked. We were able to track him as far as the hotel, but he was gone from there by the time we got there."

"That's all you have?" Clint asked.

"I'm afraid so."

"You can't even point me in a direction?"

"Ah, I think perhaps we can help you there," Mallerby said. "Would Martel have any reason to go deeper into Alaska?"

Clint stared at Mallerby, waiting for him to answer his own question, and then said, "Hell, I don't know. Maybe he's got an army of the New South waiting for him there."

"We think not."

Clint decided not to ask who "we" was.

"There is a mountain range to the east of us. Some call it the Wrangell Mountains."

"So?"

"If he goes over those mountains," Mallerby said, "he is in Canada. From there it is easy to cross the border back into the United States."

"Or," Clint added, "he could go around the mountains."

"Yes."

Mallerby was apparently not as superficial as he appeared to be.

What made more sense, Clint asked himself—for Martel to go deeper into Alaska, or double back through Canada to the United States? How desperate was he to kill Grant? The answer to that was, pretty desperate, not only to kill Grant, but to resurrect the South. Old dreams die hard.

"I guess I'll start towards the mountains in the morning," Clint said.

Mallerby seemed pleased that Clint had taken what he'd said to heart. "Excellent. I wish you luck."

"Thanks," Clint said. "I'm going to need it."

When dinner came Clint found the soup surprisingly good. There were chunks of tender beef in the broth, along with cut-up vegetables. Mallerby, on the other hand, appeared to be having a lot of trouble cutting and chewing his steak.

SEVEN

After dinner Mallerby told Clint that he had some business to attend to, so Clint asked directions to the nearest saloon and went in search of a drink and a poker game—and if a woman came along, that would be all right too. It was certainly one way to avoid spending a cold, possibly sleepless night. Of course, if he found a woman, the night might still be sleepless. . . .

The saloon was farther down the main street, and from the size of the crowd, Clint guessed that it was the only one in town. There were women there, but it was obvious that they were professionals, and if there was one rule that the Gunsmith lived by, it was never pay for a woman. If she didn't come willingly, then she wasn't worth having. He had only been tempted to break that rule once or twice, but so far had never done so.

"Whiskey," he told the bartender as he approached what turned out to be a makeshift bar. It was about six feet long and looked to have been fashioned from boards that might have been from a dismantled boardwalk.

"Comin' up," the bartender said.

There was a dirty mirror mounted on the wall behind the bar and Clint used it to survey the room. All of the tables were full and most of the standing room as well. In the mirror he watched as one of the girls took notice of him and approached him.

She was a pretty little thing, if you didn't mind the nose. Her body was trim, with round breasts and a slim waist. Her hair was blond and worn long, her eyes were green, her mouth wide and generous—and her nose was just too damn big for her. She was barely five feet tall, but her nose belonged on a woman a foot taller.

"Hello," she said, and even her voice was nice.

"Hi," he replied.

"Buy me a drink?"

"A real one, or a watered down one?"

She gave him a slight frown, then looked him up and down before answering. "You're not interested in a girl for the night, are you?"

"Definitely," he said.

"But you don't want to pay for one."

"I never pay for one," he answered, "but I will buy you a drink."

"Thanks." She called the bartender over and said, "Give me a drink on the gentleman, Leo . . . a real one."

"Okay, Kit."

He brought her a drink and she raised it in a silent toast before drinking.

"Tell me," she said then, "what do you have that most men don't?"

"What do you mean?"

"Well, most men don't mind paying for a girl for the night," she said, "or for an hour, for that matter. Since you won't, I assume you don't have to."

"I've never found it necessary," he admitted.

She looked him up and down and said, "Then my question stands. What have you got that other men don't?"

"Principles."

She laughed at that and asked, "What's your name, friend?"

"Clint."

"I'm Kit," she said.

"I heard."

She finished the drink and said, "You're in the wrong place, Clint. There ain't another soul within miles with principles."

"I won't tell anyone if you won't," he said.

"That's a deal," she said, touching his arm. "Call me if you get cold enough, huh?"

"I never get that cold."

She gave him another speculative look, as if she were really curious about him, and then said, "Well, you never know, maybe I will."

He watched the sway of her hips as she walked away from him and thought that it really was a shame about that nose. In spite of it, however, he really wouldn't have minded . . . but not for money.

"She may be little," Leo the bartender said, "but she's got a lot of energy."

Clint looked at the man and said, "No sale, friend. Just give me a beer this time."

"If you say so."

"I do."

While waiting for his beer Clint looked over at the two tables where poker games were in full swing.

"Are those regular games?" he asked when the bartender returned.

"Three or four of the players are regulars, but they're always looking for fresh blood."

"Are the games on the level?"

"Would you be able to tell if they weren't?"

Clint looked the bartender square in the eye and said, "In a minute."

The bartender studied the Gunsmith and then said, "Yeah,

I guess you could. Better play at the table on the left,'' the man said.

"Against the wall?"

"Right. It's on the level unless one of the other strangers is a mechanic."

"And the other table?"

"You just passing through, mister?" the bartender asked.

"That's right."

"Then don't ask," the other man said. "It ain't healthy."

"Has this town got a sheriff?"

"It sure does," the bartender said. "He's playing at the other table."

EIGHT

Clint decided to sit at the table that was on the level as soon as the chair he wanted opened up. He'd wait awhile, and if it didn't, he'd go to bed.

During his second beer, the man sitting with his back to the wall stood up and announced that he was through. Clint picked up his beer and moved forward through the crowd before someone else could claim it.

"Mind if I sit in?" he asked. As he did so, he saw the sheriff look up at him from the other table. He nodded at the man with the badge, who returned the nod and then went back to his cards. Clint had been able to see that the sheriff was in his early fifties, gray haired with a gray mustache and a red-veined nose. He also noticed that the man was chewing a gigantic wad of tobacco.

"Sit yourself down, sonny," one of the players said. He was as toothless as he was hairless, and Clint figured the old man had earned the right to call him "sonny."

"Thanks."

The old man explained the rules of the game, as it was already in progress, and Clint found nothing that he might object to. They were playing straight poker, table stakes.

"That's fine with me," he said, taking out some money. "Let's get on with it."

It was the old man's deal and he doled out five cards to each player for draw poker. There were six players in the

33

game and since Clint was seated to the dealer's right, he was the last to go. When all of the others declined to open, he threw in two dollars and said, "Open for two." With threes, he opened on a hunch.

Two players dropped out immediately, and the others called.

"How many?" the old man asked each one. He had been one of the players to go out.

"One," the first man said. Clint looked at the stack of money in front of the man. He was the big winner, and to have passed with two pair was greedy.

The other two players took three each, and the Gunsmith took his time deciding. Finally he threw away the two threes and said, "Two."

When they all had their cards the old man said, "To the opener."

"Five dollars," Clint said.

The man who was so far ahead that he was cocky enough to pass with two pair said, "I raise it ten."

"Ten more," the second man in the game said.

The third man let air out of his mouth and then said, "I have to call."

"I call," Clint said, "and raise it twenty."

The first man frowned and said, "I'll call."

The second player said, "I call and reraise."

The third said, "Shit, three of a kind's no good here," and threw his cards down.

"You said it, friend," the first man said. Then he looked at Clint. "It's up to you."

"I know who it's up to," Clint said. He fingered the bills on the table, counting them out. "I call and raise fifty."

"Fifty?" the first man squawked.

"Fifty," the old man repeated, grinning. "That's what the man said."

The first man glared at the old man, then counted out his cash and said, ''I call both raises.''

''This could go on all night,'' the second man said.

''Come on,'' the first man said, ''call or fold, friend.''

The second man was considerably larger than the first, and glared at him to bring that point across. When the first man averted his eyes, the second said, ''I got the winning hand, but I'm gonna call, 'cause I'm running out of money.'' He glared again and said, ''You got most of it, friend, and here's where I get some back.'' He threw the money into the pot and said, ''You're called. What've ya got?'' he asked Clint.

''I've got a full house,'' the first man said quickly, before Clint could move or speak. ''Aces full,'' he said, dropping his cards face up on the table.

He went for the pot and the second, larger man brought his hand down on both of his.

''Hold it, friend,'' he said. Laying his cards out face up he said, ''I got four Jacks, and some of my money back.''

As the second man went to rake in the pot Clint said, ''Excuse me.''

Both of the other men looked at him, and he asked, ''Remember me? I was the last raiser?''

''How you gonna beat four Jacks?'' the big man said.

''With a straight flush,'' Clint said. He laid his cards on the table, showing a heart straight flush from the six to the ten. When he had thrown away his two threes, he'd kept the seven, eight and nine of hearts, and had drawn the six and the ten.

''What?'' the man with four Jacks cried out.

The man with the full house started laughing, and after a night of losing his money to the same man, the big man had apparently had enough. Having that same man laugh at him was more than he could take.

''That's it,'' he cried out, and with a heave he overturned

the table, knocking several of the players to the floor, including the object of his anger.

The Gunsmith, on the other hand, was able to gain his feet before the table turned over, and staggered back out of the way. He watched as the sore loser drew his gun and knew that he intended to kill the big winner, who was still helpless on the floor.

"Don't do it," Clint cried out, but the man was beyond hearing. As he brought his gun to bear on the fallen man, the Gunsmith drew and fired in one incredibly swift motion. His slug went into the man's left shoulder, spinning him around and knocking him to the floor. With a look of shock on his face the man brought up the gun that he still had and aimed it at the Gunsmith, who had no choice but to fire again, striking the man in the chest.

"Damn!" he snapped, holstering his gun.

"You saved my life," the man who'd had the full house said. He staggered to his feet and said again, "You saved my life."

Clint was about to reply when he heard the sound of a revolver hammer being cocked behind him.

"Just stand steady, friend," a voice said. "This here's the law speaking."

"Sheriff, you saw—"

"I saw you kill a man, friend," the lawman said. "I want you to hand your gun back to me, and then you and me are gonna take a walk to my office."

With no choice in the matter Clint removed his gun and handed it behind him. This was one time maybe he should have gone ahead and paid for a girl. It might have saved him a lot of trouble.

NINE

Clint spent the night in a cell, and it was the coldest place he had ever been. There had been no use explaining the incident to the sheriff, because he had been right there at the next table where he couldn't have missed it. The lawman, whose name was Curry, explained to Clint that he was just the sheriff, and not a judge, and that was why Clint was in jail.

Yes, sir, the Gunsmith thought, the night in bed with the girl with the big nose, even bought and paid for, was looking better all the time. He doubted he'd even get his money back, since it had been strewn about the floor with everyone else's.

In the morning, the sheriff brought him a cup of coffee and said, "I guess you picked the wrong game to play in, huh, friend?"

"I picked the right game, Sheriff," Clint said. "At least it was on the level."

The sheriff's face went red and he was about to reply when he heard the front door open.

"I'll be back," he promised. He left the cell area to go to the front office, where he was out of Clint's sight. The coffee was weak, but at least it was hot, and that's what counted at the moment.

Clint could hear voices, but couldn't make out what was being said. From the sound of it, though, the sheriff wasn't too happy.

Presently, the lawman came back into the cellblock—which consisted of one lone cell—and unlocked the door.

"You're out, Mr. Gunsmith," he said, and Clint thought he knew what had happened. He walked out of the cell, handed the sheriff the empty cup, and walked out into the office where he found—as he'd expected—the military commander's assistant, Mr. John Mallerby.

The sheriff came out behind him and dropped his keys on the desk. "He's all yours, Mr. Mallerby, but you're the one who's gonna have to explain it to the judge."

"I'm sure Captain Walker will be able to do that with no problem, Sheriff."

"Yeah," the lawman said, sourly. He tapped Clint on the shoulder and said, "Back in Texas and such you're a big man, Mr. Gunsmith, but this is my town. Remember that."

"Believe me, Sheriff," Clint said, "you and this town deserve each other. My gun, please?"

Sheriff Curry glared at the Gunsmith, then opened a drawer in his desk and produced his gunbelt.

"Thank you," Clint said, strapping it on.

"I suggest we leave, Mr. Adams," Mallerby said.

"Lead the way, Mr. Mallerby," Clint said. "Lead the way." Outside Clint said to Mallerby, "I suppose you're wondering what happened last night?"

"Not at all," Mallerby said. "It was all explained to me."

"It was?" Clint asked. "By whom?"

"By me," a man's voice said from off to one side. Clint turned in the direction of the voice and saw the man whose life he had saved the night before.

"You saved my life, friend," the smaller man said. "I don't forget something like that."

"Mr. Estle came to me early this morning to see if I could help," Mallerby said. "When he told me what happened, I came right over."

"And none too soon either," Clint said. "It was freezing in that cell. I could do with a pot of hot coffee. Will you gentlemen join me for breakfast?"

"Fine by me," Estle said.

"I'm afraid I can't," Mallerby said. "I've got to put this into a report for Captain Walker. Will you see me before you leave, Mr. Adams?"

"Clint," the Gunsmith told him, "and I'll be glad to drop by and see you before I leave, John."

"Excellent," Mallerby said. "Enjoy your breakfast, gentlemen."

Mallerby walked off and Clint turned to Estle. As he did he remembered where his money had gone the night before.

"Uh, I was going to buy breakfast, but my money—"

"Here's your money," Estle said, handing Clint a wad of folded-up bills, "including what you won on that last hand."

Clint accepted the money, staring curiously at Estle. "How—?"

"I'm a gambler, Mr. Adams," Estle said. "I keep track of what goes on at the table. I knew how much money was yours, and how much was mine from what was dumped on the floor. The others could argue over the rest."

Shaking his head, Clint said, "Well, then, the eggs and steak are on me, after all."

"Just the eggs, thanks," Estle said. "I've tried the steak in this town."

"What could they do to eggs?" Clint asked.

"Don't ask."

TEN

They went to the same café where Clint and Mallerby had dinner the night before, and they both ordered eggs and coffee.

"The steak here is deadly," Estle said.

"I'll take your word for it."

Over breakfast Estle asked, "So what's the Gunsmith doing in Alaska?" When Clint threw him a sharp look the man said, "Well, when I went to see that fella Mallerby, he kind of let the cat out of the bag."

"No cat to let out," Clint said. "I don't make any secret about my name."

"What about the reason you're here?" Estle asked. "Is that a secret?"

"Just passing through," Clint said, with a straight face, aware of how ludicrous it sounded.

"Just passing through Alaska?" Estle said.

"What's your excuse?"

"Me?" he said. "I'm a gambler, looking for easy pickings. I thought Alaska would sort of be untouched land, if you know what I mean."

"I do. How's it going?"

"Not bad, actually. . . . Up until last night, that is."

"You get sore losers no matter where you go, don't you?" Clint asked.

"That's true, but that one last night sort of ruined things for me. It was no coincidence that I was waiting outside the jail for you. The sheriff had just finished telling me to get out of town."

"For more reasons than that, I'll bet."

Estle frowned and asked, "What do you mean?"

Clint related to Estle what the bartender had told him about the two games.

"Don't tell me you never sat at the other table."

"I make it a rule never to play poker with a lawman," Estle said. "As soon as I saw the sheriff playing at that table every night, I staked out the other one. Now that you mention it, though, I did notice that the sheriff never had a losing night."

"Didn't you ever wonder why?"

Estle shrugged and said, "I figured he just might be that good. You wouldn't expect a lawman to cheat, would you?" he asked with mock seriousness.

"Of course not," Clint said.

"So where do you head from here?" the gambler asked.

"Don't rightly know."

"Neither do I," the gambler said. "What do you say we make up our minds together?"

"That's a possibility," Clint said, careful not to commit to anything. "I have to talk to Mallerby again, but we can discuss it again later, over a drink."

"When were you planning on leaving?"

"Actually, I had planned on today, but to tell you the truth, I didn't sleep very well in that jail cell."

"Cold, huh?"

"Colder than you could imagine," Clint said. "I need a hot bath and some sleep."

"Sounds like you won't be leaving until at least tomorrow morning."

"Probably."

Estle sat back and said, "I don't know if the sheriff would sit still for me spending one more day in his fair town."

"I might be able to arrange it," Clint said, "but I doubt that you'd be able to play poker tonight."

Estle grinned across the table at Clint and said, "At least, not in the saloon."

"Where then?"

"Ah, there are places in every town—"

"Just remember—uh, I don't know your first name."

"Just call me L.D."

The look on Estle's face invited comment, but Clint merely said, "L.D., just remember what Curry said about this being his town. I think you can just about take that literally."

"You're probably right," Estle said. "Maybe you should talk to your friend Mallerby about that."

"I think John Mallerby has enough on his mind right now without taking on a sheriff with a town under his thumb."

"Do you really think so?"

"Take my word for it, L.D.," Clint said.

ELEVEN

After breakfast Clint excused himself, saying that he had some business to attend to with John Mallerby.

"I'll meet you later in the saloon for that drink, then," L.D. Estle said, "on me, of course."

"We'll see."

It was Estle who then gave Clint directions to Mallerby's office—or what he was using for an office while in town. The gambler had been in town long enough to find that out.

Clint followed the directions and found himself at the General Store.

"Kin I help ya?" a wizened old-timer asked from behind the counter.

"Yes, I'm looking for John Mallerby, the military commander's assistant."

"Upstairs," the old man said. "First door on your right."

"Thank you."

There was a doorway at the back of the store which led to the stairs, and Clint climbed them and made his first right. The door to the office was open, and he could see Mallerby sitting at an old desk that was too small for him. He was sitting sideways with his long legs out ahead of him.

"Ah, Mr. Adams," he said when he noticed Clint enter.

"You might as well call me Clint, John," the Gunsmith said. "After all, you did get me out of jail."

"Just doing my job . . . Clint," the man explained. "You couldn't very well do yours from the inside of a cell, could you?"

"No, I sure couldn't," Clint agreed.

"If you're to explain what happened last night, you needn't bother. I know all about it."

"You do?"

"Yes, according to Mr. Estle—and one of the girls at the saloon—you had no choice but to shoot or be killed, yourself."

"That isn't much of a choice."

"I quite agree."

"You seem to have looked into the matter pretty thoroughly," Clint observed.

"Well, after all, you are a representative of the United States government, and I must prepare a report on the incident."

"For whom?"

"For Captain Walker, of course," Mallerby answered. "He, in turn, will send a report to Mr. Fenton."

Clint smiled. He'd give almost anything to see the look on Fenton's face. It would almost be worth killing a man for.

No, actually, it wouldn't. Clint Adams detested killing, and was sorry that it seemed a large part of his reputation.

"Well then," Clint said, "I guess I'll just go and get myself a hot bath and some sleep."

"You won't be leaving today, then?" Mallerby asked, looking alarmed.

"John," Clint began patiently, "I didn't get much sleep in that jail cell, you know. If I go out there and fall asleep on my horse, all I'll accomplish is getting my fool head shot off. Now that wouldn't be in the best interests of the United States government, would it?"

"I daresay not," Mallerby agreed, "not when you put it that way."

"My friend," Clint said, "that's the only way there is to put it. Look for me in the café at dinner time. If we cross trails, we can eat together."

"I would enjoy that."

"See you later."

Clint left, walked down the stairs and through the store, and headed for his hotel. He felt dirtier than he had ever felt in his life, and much of that dirt and grit seemed to be in his eyes. A hot bath and a warm bed were all he was thinking about at the moment.

He paid the exorbitant amount for another bath—that was what the clerk said, "*Another* bath?"—soaked in it for a while, then scrubbed himself good and climbed out. As it turned out, the room with the tub was not far from his own room, so he braved the cold by wrapping a towel around his waist and running the few steps to his door, with his gunbelt slung over his shoulder.

As he hurriedly entered his room he realized that someone was there. As he reached for his gun the towel slipped, and he allowed it to fall to the floor in favor of palming the weapon.

"Well," the girl from the saloon said from his bed, staring at his nakedness, "I don't know whether to feel welcome," and then, staring at his gun, "or threatened."

"How'd you find my room?" he asked, hanging the gunbelt on the back of a chair.

"You're the only stranger in town," she said, shrugging her shoulders, which almost caused the sheet she was holding against her to fall away. She grabbed it, as if what she was hiding behind it was to be a surprise, revealed only when she was ready to do so.

"My name is Clint Adams," he said.

"And my name is Kit Singer."

"Hello, Kit Singer."

"Hi," she said grinning. "Now that we've been properly introduced," she added, "are you going to pick up your towel?"

He looked down at himself, as if he were surprised to find himself naked.

"Well, to tell you the truth, Kit," he said, looking at her again, "now that we've been properly introduced, I don't think I'll be needing it, do you?"

"To tell you the truth," she said, dropping the sheet to her waist, "no."

TWELVE

Her breasts were plumper than they had looked when she was dressed. The nipples were brown, and already beginning to turn into hard little pebbles.

"You look cold," she said. "Come over here and I'll warm you up."

That was an invitation the Gunsmith just couldn't pass up.

He walked to the bed and very deliberately got in with her. He pulled the sheet away so that she was totally exposed, and he could see the golden tangle of hair between her legs.

He palmed one of her breasts, enjoying the way the nipple scraped his hand, then he tweaked the nipple hard, eliciting a squeal from the girl.

"Two can play that game," she said, reaching for his swollen penis.

She ran her nails lightly along the underside, until she reached his balls, which she cupped gently, grinning mischievously at Clint.

"Don't you dare," he told her. "It will all be over before we get started."

"Well," she said, sliding her hand up his penis again, "we wouldn't want that to happen."

She closed her fist over him, trapping him in a delightful grip, and he did the same to one of her breasts. He leaned over and kissed her, and her tongue flashed into his mouth, a darting, searching thing. His hand slid from her breast, traveled over her stomach and probed into that patch of golden hair. When he found what he wanted she jumped at his touch, and moaned into his mouth.

As his fingers probed he slid his mouth away and said, "You work late. Why aren't you home sleeping?"

"You made me curious last night," she said. "I was going to wait for you here then, but then you got carted off to jail and I decided to wait until morning." He kissed her again, thrusting his tongue into her mouth at the same time as he drove his middle finger more deeply into her. She broke the kiss and gasped, "Do you want me to leave?"

"Don't be silly," he said.

She slid down so that she was lying on her back and he began to suck on her nipples while continuing to manipulate her with his hand.

"Oh God," she breathed, clutching the back of his head, crushing his face into her breasts.

He ran his tongue through the valley between her breasts, savoring the taste of her salt and skin, and then began to kiss his way down her body.

"What are you going to . . . to do—oh!"

Instead of telling her what he was going to do, he showed her.

He removed his hand and replaced it with his tongue, licking her first on the outside, and then thrusting his tongue inside of her. She picked her hips up off the bed, pressing herself tighter against his face, and he continued to devour her. Finally, he moved his tongue up and fastened his lips over her taut bud. It blossomed further as he sucked on it, and then her belly began to tremble uncontrollably, a preamble to her shattering climax.

Without giving her a chance to breathe he moved up and drove his stiff cock deep inside of her. She gasped, and reached around to cup his buttocks, digging her nails into his flesh.

"Oh yes, damn it, do it, do it hard . . . harder . . ." she babbled, but as he obliged her and drove into her harder and faster, she could no longer speak coherently. She continued to moan and cry out, and at times she even grunted with the effort of bringing her butt off the bed to meet his thrusts, but whether she spoke or moaned, it seemed to add fuel to the Gunsmith's passion.

Finally, when the muscles of her pussy began to contract on him, it was Clint Adams who groaned as she literally milked his seed from him, and then she joined him as she came for the second time.

"Will you be in town long?"

"You're lucky I got locked up last night, Kit," he answered.

She stared at him in amazement and asked, "Now why would you say that?"

"If I hadn't gotten locked up," he said, "I would have been gone by now."

"Well, by golly, I guess I am lucky," she said. "I got to satisfy my curiosity."

"And?" he asked her.

"Hey," she said, snaking her hand underneath the sheet, so she could take hold of him, "I said *satisfy*, didn't I?"

Clint finally drifted off to sleep, but after Kit Singer nuzzled him awake—the nuzzling being done below belt level—and they had another session with each other, he booted her out on her lovely little butt, explaining that he needed to get some sleep to catch up on what he missed during his night in jail. Reluctantly, Kit agreed to leave, and got up to get dressed.

"To tell you the truth," she said, while dressing, "I've got to get some more sleep myself, or I won't be at my best tonight."

"You were at your best this morning, Kit," he told her, "that's for sure."

She smiled at him and for the first time in a couple of hours, he noticed her nose. It didn't seem to be as large when he was in bed with her—or on top of her—but now that she was up and dressed, it was noticeable again.

"Will you be in for a drink later?"

"Definitely."

"And poker?" she asked, grinning.

"Definitely," he said, "not. That one hand I played last night taught me a lesson."

"I'll see you later, then," she said, and breezed out the door.

Clint lay on his back, savoring the pleasant feeling of fatigue in his loins, then turned over on his side and went to sleep.

THIRTEEN

Clint woke in the early afternoon, feeling rested, satisfied with himself, just a little hungry—and cold. The warmth left by Kit's body had long since faded, and he decided it was time to get up. When he left the hotel he headed for the livery stable to check on Duke.

"How's my horse doing?" he asked.

The livery man was in his fifties and walked with a perpetual stoop; when Clint entered the man had to look up at him.

"That big black of yours, he sure ain't bothered by the cold none."

"I guess he's pretty thick-skinned," Clint said. "I'll just go back and take a look at him."

"I'm takin' good care of him for you."

"I'm sure you are."

Clint walked to the rear of the stable where Duke's stall was, and the big black seemed to know he was there even before he saw him.

"You knew I'd come, huh, big boy?" Clint asked, patting the animal's neck affectionately. "Yeah, sure you did."

He spoke to Duke a little longer, then patted the big horse's rump and promised to take him out for some exercise real soon. The animal stared at him a little balefully, as if to say, yeah, I've heard that before.

"Tomorrow morning, big fella," Clint promised, "at the latest, okay?"

Duke turned his head away and studied the wall. With a last pat on the rump Clint left the stable, complimenting the liveryman on how well he was taking care of Duke.

"I know good horseflesh when I see it, mister," the man said, "and I know how to keep it that way."

Clint gave him some money to make sure he continued to feel that way.

Lunch was next on the agenda, only he decided to walk around the small town and see if there wasn't someplace else to eat. At one point his path crossed that of Sheriff Curry, and they eyed each other like two potential combatants.

"You still here?" the lawman demanded.

"Looks like it, doesn't it?" Clint replied.

"How soon you figure on leaving my town, Adams?"

"Just as soon as I've caught up on my sleep, Sheriff," Clint said. "Your jail isn't exactly conducive to a good night's sleep."

"That's too bad," the sheriff said. "I'll have to talk to the town council about putting in a better mattress."

"Why don't you do that, Sheriff?"

"And when I get it, you can be the first to try it out," Curry added. "What do you think of that?"

"I think I'm not going to think of it at all, Sheriff," Clint said. "It might ruin my lunch. Have a nice day."

He sidestepped the man and continued on, not giving him a chance to reply. He could almost feel Curry's murderous gaze on his back.

He continued on in his search for someplace other than the café to eat, and finally found one. It was a very small place, off the main street, and he decided to go in and try it.

There were only four tables inside, and he chose the one against the wall. An amazingly pretty young girl of about fourteen came out from the back wearing an apron and approached his table.

"Looks like I got here before the rush," he said to her.

She smiled, revealing remarkably even, white teeth and said, "You are the rush, mister. What can I get for you?"

"What's good?"

"Everything," the girl said. "My ma's the cook, and there ain't a better one in Alaska."

"Is that so?" Clint said. "Well, maybe I'd better let you suggest something."

"How about the lunch surprise?" she asked.

"What's that?"

"Well, if I told you, it wouldn't be a surprise, would it?"

"No, I guess it wouldn't. All right, bring me the lunch surprise."

"Be back in a jiffy," she said, turning on her heels and heading back to the kitchen. Clint admired the way the girl's bottom filled her jeans, and thought that in a few years this girl would be a real heartbreaker. It was too bad she was stuck in Cordova, Alaska.

While waiting for his lunch, Clint decided that when he was finished he would go and see Mallerby. If this town had a telegraph office, maybe Mallerby could send inquiries to some of the other towns between here and the Canadian border to see if Martel had passed through. That way he might be able to find out how far ahead of him Paul Martel was.

The young girl came out with her mother's specialty, which turned out to be a steak, covered with some kind of a brown sauce, onions, potatoes, carrots, green beans and home-made apple pie.

"You were right," he told the girl while she was cleaning up the table, "that was so good it must have been your mother's best dish. Give her my compliments, will you?"

"I sure will," she said, beaming. "I'm glad you liked it, 'cause I made it."

"You made that?" he asked in surprise.

"Yup."

"Then what was all that business about your mother?" he asked.

"Well, if I tell people I made it, they always seem to feel they have to say something nice, even if they didn't like it."

"How could anybody not like that?" he asked.

"Everybody's got different tastes," she said with a shrug.

"So, do you run this place all alone?" he asked.

"Just about. My grandfather used to do it, but he ain't up to it no more. He sits upstairs now, with a bad case of arthritis."

"I'm sorry."

"Don't be," she said. "Gramps is happy. He sits up there all day reading dime novels about all the famous gunfighters. Wild Bill Hickok, Ben Thompson, Clay Allison, the Gunsmith—you name him, and Gramps has read about him."

"Wild Bill Hickok and the Gunsmith, huh?"

"Yes, sir. Gramps says they cleaned out Abilene back in seventy-three—or was it seventy-four?" she said, frowning as she tried to remember.

"It doesn't matter, really," Clint said. "Did you make the coffee too?" he asked, changing the subject.

"Sure did."

"I'd like another pot, please," he said. "I'm a coffee man, and you make it just the way I like it."

"Coming up," she said, and bounced happily back to the kitchen.

After Clint had finished his second pot of coffee, he paid his check, and tipped the girl generously.

"Golly, mister," she said, wide-eyed, "that's almost as much as the meal itself."

"That's okay," he assured her. "You deserve it."

"Thanks."

"Don't mention it," he said, putting on his hat and starting for the door.

"Mister—" she called after him.

"Yes?"

"What's your name?"

"What's yours?"

"Wilma Sue Best," she said.

"Well, Wilma Sue," he said, watching her face for her reaction, "my name is Clint Adams."

"Clint Adams," she repeated, but from the look on her face, it didn't mean a thing to her.

"Have a good day, Wilma Sue," he said.

"You too . . . Clint."

Clint left the little restaurant, hoping that he would be able to leave town before she got around to telling her grandfather his name.

FOURTEEN

Clint went over to the general store and up the steps to John Mallerby's office. The military commander's assistant was there, bent over his desk, working on something with absolute concentration.

"That your report?" Clint asked.

"What—?" Mallerby said, jerking his head up. He looked at Clint wide-eyed for a few seconds before he was able to focus and recognize him. "Oh, Mr. Adams—Clint. Yes, I'm just finishing it up."

"Good," Clint said. "There's something I'd like you to do for me, if you will."

"Of course," Mallerby said, putting down his quill pen. "I am here to assist you."

"Fine," Clint said, and then went on to explain what he wanted Mallerby to do.

"Well, we do have a telegraph key in this town," Mallerby admitted, "and there are a few between here and the Canadian border. I suppose I could do that."

"Good," Clint said, "and I think the sooner the better. Before I leave maybe we could know what two points he's in between, where he passed last, and where he hasn't reached yet."

"I'm sure we can," Mallerby said, picking up his pen again. "Just let me finish this up and I'll get right to it."

"Fine."

"Where will you be?"

"In the saloon, I suppose."

"The, uh, saloon where you were forced to shoot that man?"

"Is there another saloon in town?"

"No."

"Then that's the one I'll be at."

"Of course."

"Don't worry, John," Clint said. "I'll try my best not to shoot anyone tonight. I promise." He raised his right hand to enforce his promise.

"No, of course you wouldn't . . . shoot anyone," Mallerby stammered. "I'll just, uh, finish—"

"Okay, John," Clint said. "I'll be waiting to hear from you."

"Yes, fine," Mallerby said, and went back to his report. His concentration, however, was not as absolute as it had been moments before.

He could hear Clint going down the steps, and when he thought he'd reached the bottom he got up and walked to the window, which overlooked the main street. He saw Clint leave the store and head for the saloon.

He walked back to his desk, looked at what he'd been writing, then crumpled it up, grabbed his hat, and left the office.

Mallerby left the store and walked down the street to the hole-in-the-wall telegraph office.

"Can I help you?" the clerk asked.

"I'd like to send a telegram."

"Sure," the man said. He grabbed a pad and pencil and prepared to write. "How many telegrams you want to send, sir?"

"One," Mallerby said. "Just one."

FIFTEEN

Clint went directly to the saloon, which was less crowded in the afternoon than it had been the night before. L.D. Estle was standing at the bar with a beer, looking longingly at a three-handed poker game that was going on in a corner.

"Forget it," Clint said, standing next to the gambler. "Beer," he told the bartender.

"I can dream, can't I?" Estle asked.

"You can," Clint said, accepting his beer from the bartender. "What happened to your back-room game?"

Estle snorted and said, "Curry really does have this town sewed up. There are only two games in this town, and they both take place in here. He runs one table, and cuts the pot on the other."

"Not last night," Clint said.

Estle grinned and said, "No, he didn't have a chance to cut it last night, that's for sure."

"Besides, if he had tried, you wouldn't have taken kindly to it, and you might have gotten yourself in a lot of trouble."

"I *would* have gotten myself into a lot of trouble," Estle said. "And speaking of trouble . . ."

"What about it?"

"You might have some riding your way."

"How so?"

"Well, that fella you killed last night? It turns out he's got some relatives who live hereabouts."

"How many is some?" Clint asked.

"Brothers," Estle said, and then held up his fingers. "Four of 'em."

"God damn it," Clint swore. "Why does every saddle tramp who thinks he can solve an argument with a gun always seem to have a big family?"

"Maybe he gets used to solving his arguments that way," Estle said. "Way I hear it, he was the baby of the family."

"The baby?" Clint said. "I'd hate to see what the rest of them look like."

"Guess it's a lucky thing we're leaving town together tomorrow," Estle said.

"You're leaving town tomorrow," Clint asked, "with me?"

"Well, hell," Estle said, "whose life were you saving when you shot that fella?"

"Yours."

"Well, then, his brothers ain't going to take any more kindly to me than they do to you."

"You've got a point there."

"We can ride out together and then head our own ways, if that's what you want. I'm just looking to get an early start, same as you."

"Well," Clint said, "that sounds all right to me, but what do we do to while away the hours tonight?"

Estle glanced at Clint and then said, "I've got a deck of cards. Brand new, never been opened."

"Yeah?" Clint said, giving the gambler a wary look.

"Honest to God," Estle said, producing the desk so that Clint could see that they were sealed.

"What are you proposing?" Clint asked. "Two-handed solitaire?"

"Or head to head poker, just you and me," Estle said. "Small stakes, just to pass the time."

"And what do you think Curry will have to say about that?" Clint asked.

"What can he say if we don't let anyone else into the game?" Estle asked.

"Nothing, I guess," Clint said. "All right, let's get those beers and a corner table."

They ordered two more beers from the bartender, then staked out a corner table. Estle broke the seal on the cards, shuffled them up, and dealt out two hands of five card draw. In half an hour, there was a crowd of people gathered around the table, watching two good poker players at work.

"If I knew you were this good," Estle said, "I'd have suggested higher stakes."

"Just play," Clint said. "I know you're a gambler, don't make me think you're a con man, too."

"Me?" Estle said, feigning shock.

"How many cards do you want?" Clint asked.

"I'll take one," Estle said. Clint dealt him the one, then examined his own hand again.

"I'll take one," he said finally, discarding a card and dealing himself a new one. "The bet's yours."

"I'll bet four bits," Estle said, tossing the money into the pot.

"I'll call," Clint said, "and raise it four bits."

Estle examined Clint's cards, running the ball of his index fingers over the edge of one of his end cards. It was something he did all the time, Clint had noticed, and did not give an indication of whether he had a good hand or a bad one.

"I'm going to call you, Clint," Estle said, "only because you're almost as good a card player as I am."

Estle threw the extra four bits into the pot and then said, "What do you have?"

At that point the batwing doors to the saloon flew open with a bang and four men stepped through. As they entered, one behind the other, you could see that each man was larger than the one before him. When they were all inside, they seemed to fill the room.

The crowd around the poker table turned to examine the men who had entered. Clint, with his back to the wall, was able to see them also, while Estle continued to look at Clint.

"We're looking for the man who killed our brother," one of the men said in a loud voice.

"And if we don't find him right quick," one of the other men said, "we're gonna start doing some killin' of our own until we do."

Estle looked at Clint's face, pursed his lips and raised his eyebrows.

"Are we in trouble?" he asked in a low voice.

"Now where is he?" the first man bellowed, and suddenly the crowd that had been around the poker table melted away. It was as if everyone in the room had suddenly pointed a finger at the two men seated at the table.

"I guess we're in trouble," Clint said.

SIXTEEN

Clint put his cards down flat on the table, and Estle followed his example. The men at the door were all looking their way now.

"Which one of you killed our brother?" one of them said. At this point, if you didn't watch their mouths very carefully, you'd be hard put to tell which one was doing the talking. They all had the same bass rumble that seemed to originate deep down inside their barrel chests.

Before Clint had a chance to speak, Estle turned around and said, "We both did."

That confused the brothers, and they turned to look at one another.

"We heard that one man shot him," one said.

"He pulled his gun on me—" Estle said, and then Clint cut in quickly before he could finish and said, "—and I shot him."

Now it was clearer to them.

"You're the one we want," one of the brothers said to Clint.

"We're a matched set," Estle said. He and Clint both stood up now, so that their hands were clear of the table. "If you want one, you got to take the other."

The brothers looked at each other again and it was as if they had communicated without speaking.

"We'll take both," one of them said, and then they all went for their guns.

65

The Gunsmith's gun came out before anyone's, and he put a bullet into the left shoulder of the brother who had been doing most of the talking.

Estle flicked his arm up, and a derringer sprang into his hand from inside his sleeve. He fired once, striking one of the brothers in the upper thigh with a .41-caliber bullet.

None of the brothers had yet cleared leather, and now the remaining two uninjured men weren't sure they wanted to. The one shot in the shoulder lurched against one of the uninjured ones, and the other healthy man caught the brother who had been shot in the thigh before he could fall.

"Okay," Clint announced loudly. "What happened to your brother was unfortunate, but he gave me no choice. I'm giving you boys a chance. Either go for your guns, or clear out."

He holstered his gun, but Estle—who was better with a deck of cards than he was with his gun—kept his handy, even though there was only one shot left in it.

The brothers once again communicated without speaking, and then the two healthy ones, half carrying, half dragging the others, left the saloon.

Estle replaced his derringer and turned to face Clint, who was staring down at the table with a strange look on his face.

"I guess we can get back to our game now," L.D. said.

Clint looked at Estle, who thought that his new friend's eyes were a bit out of focus.

"The hand is yours," Clint said suddenly. "I'm going to get a drink."

Clint strode to the bar without touching his cards again, and Estle stared after him, wondering what was wrong. He looked down at Clint's hand, then reached over and turned the cards face up.

The Gunsmith had been sitting with aces and eights, the hand Bill Hickok had been holding when he was killed.

SEVENTEEN

Estle gathered his cards together—and his money—and followed Clint to the bar.

"Want one?" Clint asked, indicating the whiskey in his hand.

"I'll stick with beer," Estle said, and signaled the bartender for one.

The gambler watched as Clint Adams tossed off the whiskey, and then ordered a beer. If Clint had ordered another whiskey, Estle would have been worried.

"Old memories?" he asked.

Clint looked at the gambler, then said, "Yeah, old memories, better left behind."

"They usually are," Estle agreed.

Before they could continue, Sheriff Curry walked in, looking around the room suspiciously until his eyes settled on Clint and Estle.

"You two," he said, advancing on them.

"Us?" Estle asked.

"What the hell went on here?" Curry demanded.

"When?" Clint asked.

"Just now," Curry said. "I heard shooting."

"Shooting?" Clint asked.

"And I saw some men riding away. Some of them looked hurt. I want to know what was going on."

"Did someone make a complaint?" Estle asked.

"No—"

"Then I don't see where you have a problem, Sheriff," Clint said. "We're just having a drink and killing some time until we leave in the morning."

"You're both leaving?"

"Together," Estle said. "We're killing two birds with one stone for you."

"Well, see that you do," Curry said. "If I see either of you here after tomorrow, I'll be on your ass like a fly on molasses."

"That's clever," Estle said.

"I'd write it down if I had a piece of paper," Clint said.

"Just see that you're out of town," Curry said. He glared at them for emphasis, and then left.

"He'll find out what went on," Estle said.

"So what?" Clint said. "We'll be out of town by then, and he'll be the least of our worries."

Estle studied Clint, and was glad to see that his friend seemed to have shaken off his earlier mood.

"You're pretty good with that derringer," Clint observed.

"Not as good as you are with that gun of yours," Estle answered. "I assume you were aiming for the shoulder."

"Definitely," Clint said. "They were slow enough for me to decide that I didn't have to kill any of them. What about you? That was a nicely placed shot."

"Uh, yeah," Estle said, looking embarrassed. "Well, the guy did have a thigh the size of a tree trunk, and I wish I could say I was aiming for it. The truth is, I'm a lot better with cards then I am with a gun, and that derringer is really for over the table work."

"You weren't aiming for the thigh."

"I . . . hurried the shot," the gambler said. "The fact of the matter is, I'm lucky I hit anything."

"I guess we're both lucky," Clint said, putting his hand on Estle's shoulder. "Don't worry about it."

"I won't," Estle said. "I saw that move of yours. I have the feeling you would have been able to handle it all by yourself if I hadn't been there."

"Possibly," Clint said.

"Now, what do we do to pass the rest of the evening?" Estle asked.

At that moment Kit Singer came down the stairs, dressed for work.

"Does that give you any ideas?" Clint asked.

Estle looked over at the girl and said, "Not bad, if it wasn't for that nose."

"Find one that better suits your taste, then," Clint suggested. "Why don't we have dinner later? I found a place that beats the café all to hell."

"I'm for that," Estle said. "My stomach hasn't yet forgiven me for bringing it to this godforsaken place."

"Why don't you just book passage and get out of here, then?" Clint asked.

"Uh, I'd rather take a little more time getting back," Estle said, evasively. For the first time, Clint seemed to sense a reluctance on Estle's part to return to the civilized world, for reasons of his own. Clint decided not to pry.

"Well, I guess I could use the company."

"Don't sound so enthusiastic," Estle said. "Look, if there's some reason you don't want me to ride along with you—"

"When I come up with a reason, L.D.," Clint said, interrupting him, "I'll let you know. Fair enough?"

Estle thought a moment, then said, "Fair enough."

EIGHTEEN

"This little girl's name is Wilma Sue," Clint told Estle as Wilma Sue came to their table to serve them, "and she is the best cook I've ever run across."

"Really?" Estle said, looking the girl over. "She's pretty too," he said.

"Thank you both," Wilma Sue said, with a curtsy. "Did either of you come here to eat?"

"We both did," Clint said.

Looking around at the empty room Estle added, "Doesn't look like anyone else did, though."

"That just means we beat the rush," Clint said. He looked at Wilma Sue and said, "Surprise us, sweetheart."

"Pleasantly," Estle added.

"Of course," she said, making a face at him. He watched her saucy little bottom as she walked to the kitchen, then looked at Clint and smiled.

"Forget it," Clint said.

"Forget what?"

"Whatever you were thinking."

Estle was at least ten years younger than Clint, which still made him too old for Wilma Sue. The first time Clint had seen her he guessed her age at about fourteen, but now he was upgrading it. She could have been sixteen, but there were still too many years between her and the gambler.

"What did you think I was thinking?"

"What men usually think when they see a pretty woman," Clint said. "She's too young."

"She's seventeen or eighteen, at least," Estle said. "That's plenty old enough."

"She's younger than that," Clint said. "She can't be more than fifteen."

Estle frowned his disagreement and said, "We'll ask her."

"You ask her," Clint said. "Either way she's too young for me."

"Must be hell getting old, huh?"

"Why," Clint asked, "you're not?"

Wilma Sue brought them each a bowl of steaming stew and a mug of beer, and then went back to the kitchen without being asked her age.

"What happened?" Clint asked.

"I chickened out," Estle said. He tasted the stew, then looked at Clint with raised eyebrows.

"Surprised?"

"Pleasantly," the gambler said, taking another bite.

At that point Wilma Sue came out with some chunks of bread and said, "Soak up the gravy with these."

"Thank you," Clint said.

"This is very good," Estle told her.

She looked him straight in the eye and said, "I know."

When she walked away from them there was a deliberate sway to her hips, and Clint thought that perhaps Estle was right. She just might have been old enough.

"This is really good," Clint said. "I wonder why there's no one else eating here. It sure beats the food at that other place."

"Yes," Clint said, "I've wondered about that myself."

"People have to have a reason not to come here," Estle said. "Who works here with her?"

"It used to be her grandfather, but he's sick now. He sits upstairs reading about the legends of the West."

"That would include you, wouldn't it?" Estle asked.

"So I've been told," Clint replied.

"How does it feel to be a legend?"

"I don't think about it," Clint said, "and I never talk about it. If you want to ride out of here with me in the morning, you'd do well to remember that."

Estle paused over his food and stared at Clint to see if he was serious. When he saw that he was he said, "All right, consider it remembered."

"Thank you," Clint said, and then in a lighter tone. "Now eat your food, will you? You don't want to insult Wilma Sue."

"That's the last thing I'd want to do."

After dinner they left the place together, but stopped outside to sort out their separate ways.

"Where are you off to?"

"I've got to see Mallerby," Clint said, "and then I'll probably go over to the saloon."

"Cards, or women?" Estle asked.

"I've had enough cards," Clint said.

"And women?"

Clint smiled and said, "Never enough."

"That's funny."

"What is?"

"I feel the same way about cards."

That may have been so, but as Clint walked away he looked back and saw Estle going back into the restaurant— and he didn't figure he was going in to ask Wilma Sue to play cards.

Clint found John Mallerby in his office, bent over his desk again.

"You always work this hard?" he asked.

"I work the only way I know how," Mallerby said, looking up.

"I'm sure," Clint said. "Were you able to do what I asked you to do?"

"Of course," Mallerby said. "Martel is between here and a town called Glenallen."

"Where is that?"

"At the base of the Wrangell Mountains," Mallerby said. "It should take you five days to get there."

"Five days?"

"That is, if you knew where you were going."

"What do you suggest?"

"A guide."

"Do you know any?"

"I do."

"Can you have him ready by tomorrow morning?" Clint asked.

"I'm sure I could."

"The United States government will foot the bill," Clint said.

"Of course."

"Tell him that if he gets me there in four, there's a bonus in it for him," Clint said. "Where's the last place Martel was seen?"

"A man fitting his description was seen in Copper Center," Mallerby answered. "He has not yet reached Glenallen."

"All right," Clint said, "at least now I have a destination. What happens after Glenallen?"

"If he's going to Canada he'll hug the base of the mountains," Mallerby said. "After that he'll reach Northway, and from there he'll go directly to the Yukon Territory of Canada."

"You've been a big help, John," Clint told Mallerby, which was something of a surprise to both of them—to Mallerby that Clint would say that, and to Clint that it was true.

"You've practically given me a map, and I appreciate it," Clint added.

"I'm doing my job, Clint," Mallerby said, "nothing more."

"Well, I just want you to know I appreciate it."

"I will have the guide meet you at your hotel in the morning," Mallerby said.

"I'd like to get started as the sun comes up, if you can arrange it that quickly."

"There won't be any problem with that, I assure you," Mallerby said.

"Then I guess that's all," Clint said. "I'll let you get back to your work."

"Good luck, Clint," Mallerby said.

"Thank you."

Neither man offered to shake hands, and Clint simply turned and left the office.

Once again Mallerby went to the window to watch Clint Adams walk down the street, and then he turned and walked back to his desk. He crumpled the piece of paper he'd been writing on, then turned and left the room to arrange for the guide.

Clint went to the saloon and did not find Estle waiting for him there. He did, however, find Kit Singer, who was more than eager to leave work a little early and go back to his hotel with him—free of charge, of course.

NINETEEN

Clint woke up the following morning with Kit Singer right beside him—which, considering she'd been either atop him or beneath him most of the night—was a switch. He stared at her naked back for a few moments, then moved the sheet down so that her butt was naked, and gave her a smack on the right cheek.

"What—?" she cried out, looking around, eyes wide, but still clouded by sleep. When she focused on him she said, "What the hell did you do that for?"

"It's time for me to get going," he said.

"Oh, yeah?"

"I thought you'd want one last opportunity to say goodbye before I left," he said.

She pushed herself up on her elbows and said, "Oh, you did, huh?"

"Of course, if not—" he said, starting to swing his legs off the bed.

"Wait," she said, throwing her arms around his waist and holding him back.

"Well?" he asked.

She sat up and stared him in the eye.

"What do you think of my nose?" she asked.

"I think it's too big," he said.

She pushed him down on the bed, straddled him and

77

stuffed his semi-erect penis inside of her. Moving her hips, she enjoyed the feeling of having him swell inside of her, filling her up.

She put her hands on his shoulders and dangled her breasts in his face, so he could lick and suckle her nipples.

"Is this a reward for telling you your nose was too big?" he asked.

"You're the first man who hasn't lied to me about it and told me it looked all right," she said. "You're going to have a good-bye you'll remember for a long, long time."

The guide sent by Mallerby turned out to be a Tlingit Indian, one of the tribes that inhabited the northern part of Alaska.

The man sat tall upon his horse, and had wrapped around him an odd looking blanket which Clint would later find out was called a chilkat blanket, and had been woven from cedar bark and the hair of the wild mountain goat.

The guide's name was Chooka, and Clint found it odd that he had a mustache and beard. He had never seen an Indian with facial hair before.

"I am Chooka," the man said as Clint exited the hotel. He sat astride his horse, staring down at Clint with something of a regal attitude.

"The guide?" Clint asked, and Chooka nodded.

Estle, who had been staying in a rooming house at the other end of town, came walking up to them.

"This is our guide, Chooka," Clint said. "This man will also be traveling with us," he told the guide.

Chooka shrugged, and said nothing.

"A bearded Indian?" Estle asked aloud.

"It is cold in the north," Chooka said. "There are many ways to combat it."

"Well, I hope you'll show us some," Estle said, and the Indian guide merely shrugged.

"Wait here, Chooka," Clint said. "L.D. and I will get our horses and meet you here."

"As you wish."

As they walked to the livery Estle said, "Where did you get him?"

"From Mallerby. He suggested we have a guide if we were riding to Canada."

"Is that where we're going?"

"That's where I'm heading," Clint said. "I don't know whether I'll get there or not."

"That doesn't sound encouraging," Estle said.

"I simply mean that I may finish what I'm doing before I reach the Yukon border."

"Whatever that is," Estle said.

Clint looked at the gambler and said, "I'll tell you what. When you're ready to confide in me, I'll confide in you."

"What do you mean?"

Clint paused a few beats, then said, "Just let me know."

Estle looked at the ground as they continued to walk to the livery, and when they reached it, Clint decided to lighten things up.

"Didn't see you in the saloon last night."

"I never made it," Estle said, looking up. "I went back in to see Wilma Sue and . . ."

"And you found out how old she is?" Clint asked.

Estle smiled and said, "She was old enough."

Clint grinned back and said, "Come on, let's get these animals saddled. The sheriff will be looking for us any minute."

"After what Wilma Sue told me, I might not mind that," the gambler said.

"What do you mean?"

"I think I'd better tell you once we're safely away from here," Estle said. "You might not want to leave."

"I have to leave," Clint said, frowning.

"Then all the more reason I should wait to tell you," Estle said. "After I do, and after you finish what you have to do, if you want to come back, I'll come with you."

"And if I don't want to come back?"

"I'll come back alone," Estle said. "But if you don't come back with me, then you aren't the man I think you are—and I think you are."

"I wish I knew what this was all about," Clint said, pulling the cinch tight on Duke's saddle.

"You will," Estle said, looking at Clint over his good-looking roan's back.

Clint decided not to pursue it. Estle would tell him about it soon enough, and he had other things on his mind right now.

He mounted up and said, "Let's get going, then."

Estle mounted his roan, and his eyes swept over Duke's lines in silent admiration.

"I hope I can keep up," he said.

Clint looked at the little roan and recognized the power inside the animal's small frame and said, "Don't worry, you will."

"Let's go, then."

They rode to the hotel, where their Tlingit guide waited patiently.

"Do you know where we want to go?" Clint asked.

The Indian nodded.

"Lead the way, then," Clint said. "I've wasted enough time already."

The Indian pulled his pony around and started off, and Clint and Estle fell in behind him.

With the map inside his head, and a competent guide, Clint felt for the first time that the search for Paul Martel might not be so hopeless after all.

As they put the town of Cordova behind them—for good,

he would have thought, had it not been for Loren Estle's mystifying words—Clint wondered what Ulysses S. Grant and Fenton expected him to do once he'd found Paul Martel.

"We don't want him to be able to try something like this ever again," was the way Fenton had put it.

Given Fenton's proclivity for never quite saying what he meant, that could mean they wanted Clint to kill Martel on sight. If that were the case, they were expecting too much from him.

The Gunsmith would never hesitate to kill a man if the situation warranted it, but he would never kill a man in cold blood, not even for his country.

TWENTY

"This man doesn't get tired," Estle complained. They were a half a day out of Cordova, and Chooka had given no sign of stopping.

"He's an Indian," Clint said. "A funny looking one, but still an Indian."

"You know, I never even thought about Indians being in Alaska," Estle said. "I guess they're all over."

"I guess," Clint said. "I'd also guess that, like everywhere else I've been, they were here first."

"Yeah," his companion said.

"Chooka!" Clint called.

The Indian stopped and turned to look at the Gunsmith.

"We'd like a short rest for our animals."

Chooka pointedly examined both men's mounts, then looked at Clint and said, "Your animals do not need a rest—especially not yours."

"That may be so," Clint said, "but we'd like a short rest anyway."

The Indian shrugged and turned around. He gave no indication that he would dismount, but neither did he start his horse moving. Apparently he would wait for them right where he was.

Estle dismounted and said to Clint, "He speaks pretty good English, doesn't he?"

"I was thinking the same thing," Clint said, dropping

down from Duke's back. "He doesn't speak often, but when he does it's in very good English."

Estle was examining his horse, and Clint rubbed Duke's nose and said, "You don't need a rest, do you, big boy? You like this cold, don't you?"

Duke exhaled on Clint's hand, warming it with a rush of air from his nostrils.

"I wish I had a pair of gloves," Estle said.

"You don't?"

"A gambler doesn't get much use out of gloves, Clint," the other man replied. "I've got to feel the cards, you know?"

"I've got a pair in my saddlebags," Clint said. "Come to think of it, I don't get much use out of them myself."

"I'll pick up a pair at the next town," Estle said, "if my hands don't fall off by then."

"Chooka!" Clint called.

The Indian turned and said, "Yes."

"What's the next town?"

"If we continue north we will come to Copper Center. To the west is Valdez, but we will bypass that place."

"Why?" Estle asked.

"It is out of the way."

"It's the closest town to Cordova, though, isn't it?" Clint asked.

"In distance, yes, but going there takes us away from the mountains."

Estle interrupted Clint before he could continue.

"Forget it, Clint," he said. "Whatever you have to do, you can't afford a sidetrip just to get me a pair of gloves."

"I have a scarf you can wrap your hands in," Clint said.

"Fine. That should do it until we reach Copper Center," the gambler said.

"Sounds like a mining town," Clint said.

"Should be plenty of pairs of gloves there, eh?" Estle said.

"I suppose," Clint said. "Come on, let's get moving."

They mounted up and Clint told Chooka to go ahead.

"Want to tell me what you were talking about in town?" Clint asked.

"Oh, that," Estle said. "Burns me up just to think about it."

"What, for Christ's sake?"

"The reason nobody eats at her restaurant."

"Which is?" Clint asked, patiently.

"Curry."

"What's he got to do with it?"

"Seems he and the old man—her grandfather—had a falling out not long ago."

"Over what?"

"Wilma Sue."

"What?"

"Curry took a shine to the way she was growing up, and her grandfather called him on it. Told him that if he touched her, he'd kill him."

"I guess that would put him on Curry's wrong side."

"That was a year ago," Estle said, "and now the only customers they get are strangers in town, like us. Nobody even recommends the place, for fear of getting on the wrong side of Curry."

"Sounds more like a town boss than a sheriff," Clint said. "Something should be done about him."

"My sentiments, exactly."

The tone of Estle's voice caused Clint to look over at him. The look on the gambler's face was expectant.

"Now wait a minute—" Clint began.

"Hey, I'm just a gambler, Clint," Estle said. "I can't do much beyond maybe winning the town from him."

"That might not be a bad idea," Clint said.

"It's a terrible idea."

"Give it some thought," Clint suggested. "Don't discount it until you give it some thought. Have you ever won a town in a poker game before?"

"No, but he doesn't own the town—"

"Doesn't he?"

"Not legally—"

"When did that ever stop a man like Curry?" Clint asked.

"You know," Estle said, "I could almost believe that you're serious."

"I am."

"It is a thought," Estle said, looking pensive.

"It could work, if you play it right."

"And how would I do that?"

"All you'd have to do is take the man for everything he's got, and then put it all on the line. If he wins he gets it all, and if he loses—"

"He leaves town."

"Right."

"How would I get him to abide by that though?"

Clint looked at Estle, and then said, "We'll talk about it."

TWENTY-ONE

When they camped for the night Clint built a fire and he and Estle huddled by it for warmth. Chooka, on the other hand, sat apart from them, wrapped in his Chilkat, and seemed totally unmindful of the cold.

"That must be one hell of a blanket," Estle said.

"Either that, or that Indian has incredibly thick skin."

"And warm blood."

"Right."

The smell of coffee filled the air and Clint poured himself and Estle a cup. Chooka refused when offered a cup.

"Do you think he'll eat anything?" Estle asked, as Clint moved the bacon around in the skillet.

"Only one way to find out," Clint said.

They offered, and the Indian refused.

"Good," Estle said. "More for us."

They made a meal out of bread and bacon, scooping the thick bacon grease out of the skillet with the bread. Not wanting to be slowed down by a packhorse, Clint and Estle had simply packed their saddlebags with provisions, and each had also looped a canvas bag filled with necessities around their saddle horn. Eating light would enable them to reach the next town without running out.

After dinner, when they were each having their first cup of coffee from the second pot, Estle leaned back on his elbows and said, "I'm ready."

"Ready for what?" Clint asked.

"To confide in you."

"Oh."

"We made a deal, remember?"

"I remember."

"I'm about to hold up my end of it."

"Good."

"I expect you to hold up your end, as well."

"Of course."

Estle took a deep breath—preparatory to baring his soul, obviously—and then let it out, his big secret. "I'm hiding from a woman."

Clint stared at him, wondering if he was telling the truth. "A woman," he said.

"Right," Estle said. "Let me tell you about it before you pass judgment."

"I don't intend to pass judgment."

"All right, but you'll have an opinion."

"I suppose."

"Here's the story. A few months back I met a woman in Wyoming, and we got involved."

"That's been known to happen."

"No, we really got involved," Estle said. "In fact, at one point I thought I wanted to marry the girl."

"And then you changed your mind."

"Right."

"And her father was a powerful man, and she had a couple of brothers, and maybe some cousins—"

"That's not it at all," Estle said, waving a hand.

"It's not?"

"No," he said. "Actually, her father was kind of powerful, but she didn't have any brothers or cousins."

"What then?"

"She's got four sisters, each one bigger and uglier than the other."

"And what about her?"

"Oh, don't get me wrong," Estle said. "She's a pretty girl, it's just that I couldn't see myself marrying into that family. Can you imagine having to look at her relatives all the time?"

"Why would you want to?"

"It was her idea that we live with her father and sisters after we got married."

"And that cinched it, huh?"

"You said it. I wanted out. When I told her I was leaving she got all upset, and her father and sisters started looking for me." He looked down into his cup and said, "I had to shoot her old man, and I guess they're still looking for me."

"Did you kill him?"

"No, I shot him in the shoulder. I doubt that he's dead."

"Is the law after you?"

"That I don't know," the gambler said.

"Well, I've still got a few friends who wear badges," Clint said. "Maybe when this is over we can find out for you."

"Hey, that would be great," Estle said. "I'd sure appreciate that."

"No trouble."

"Uh, what will you do if I am wanted by the law?" Estle asked then.

"Tell you."

"You won't bring me back?"

"I'm not a lawman anymore, L.D.," Clint reminded him. "There'd be no reason for me to take you back."

"I'm glad to hear that," Estle said. "Now, what about your story?"

Clint looked at Estle and said, "I really am in no position to tell you all of it."

"We had a deal."

"I'll tell you what I can," Clint said. "I'm looking for a man."

"Looking," Estle said, "or hunting?"

"Hunting, I guess," Clint said. "He tried to kill someone, and I'm supposed to catch him so that he can't try it again."

"Who did he try to kill?"

"I can't tell you that."

"Can't, or won't?"

"I'm not at liberty to," Clint said. "I've told you what I'm doing in Alaska. That holds up my end of the deal."

"Well, I can't argue that," Estle said. He finished what was left in his coffee cup, and dumped the dregs into the fire.

"Shall we leave our Indian friend on watch?" Estle asked.

"No," Clint said. "I don't think so. Let's split the watches in two, for now."

"You don't trust Chooka?"

"Let's just say I don't have any reason to right now," Clint said. "I'll take the first watch and wake you in four hours."

TWENTY-TWO

The night passed without incident. Chooka sat the whole time wrapped in his blanket with his back to them, so that neither Clint nor Estle had been able to tell if he had been asleep or awake at any time during their respective watches. In the morning, however, Chooka did not seem any the worse for wear.

"Jesus, I'm cold," Estle said when he and Clint were saddling their horses.

"I'll give you that scarf for your hands," Clint said. "It might help."

"I hope so."

Clint pulled on his gloves, passed Estle the scarf, which he wrapped around his hands, and then signaled the Indian that they were ready to proceed.

They rode in silence for a while, and then Estle asked, "Have you been deputized, or something?"

"Why do you ask?"

"Well, if you're hunting someone who tried to commit murder, you would probably have to have some kind of legal standing, wouldn't you?"

"I haven't been deputized," Clint said. "In fact, I haven't pinned on a badge for some time now, and I don't intend to."

"Sorry," Estle said. "I guess my curiosity got the better of me."

"That's all right," Clint said. "If we ride together long enough, you'll have the whole story soon enough."

"I guess I can wait, then," Estle said.

"I guess you'll have to."

They rode that entire day without incident, and that evening Chooka told them that they would be in Copper Center by midday the following day. He then went and sat away from them again, with his back to them.

"He's a strange one," Estle said. "Stranger than most Indians, I think."

"How many Indians have you known?" Clint asked.

"Not a whole hell of a lot," Estle admitted. "How many have you known?"

"A few," Clint said. "I met Quanah Parker, once," he said, remembering that incident with something less than fondness.*

"Get to be friends?"

"Hardly," he answered, "but I think we ended up respecting each other."

"Quanah Parker, himself, huh?" Estle said. "I'm very impressed."

"Don't be."

Clint stirred the beans in the pan, and Estle took out the bread and coffee.

"I'd sure like to have some of Wilma Sue's cooking about now," Clint said.

Estle grinned and said, "I'd sure like to have some of Wilma Sue right now—especially the warm parts."

"How old is she, anyway?" Clint asked.

"Wouldn't you like to know," Estle said, putting the coffee into the coffeepot.

---

*The Gunsmith #8: Quanah's Revenge

"You want some of these hot beans?"

"Sure. She's eighteen."

"She looks younger."

"Even undressed," Estle said, "but she's a sweet girl."

"Here," Clint said, pouring half of the beans out onto a plate for Estle and handing it to him. "Make do with these."

"Thanks."

Estle tore a hunk of bread in half and handed one part to Clint, and both men settled down to eat.

"Too bad one of us didn't think of bringing a bottle of whiskey along," Clint said, toward the end of their meal. "It sure would cut into this cold some."

"Say no more," Estle said. He reached into his saddlebag and brought out a full, unopened bottle of whiskey.

"I knew you'd come in handy," Clint said, extending his empty coffee cup. Estle opened the bottle and poured each one of them half a cup.

"Better put it away," Clint said. "If it works too well we'll both want more."

"What's wrong with that?"

"We've got to be alert," Clint said.

Estle nodded, capped the bottle, and put it away. "You don't think we should have offered some to Chooka?"

"That's right," Clint said. "I don't think."

Clint took a sip of the whiskey, and it cut through the cold, all right, and built a small fire in the pit of his stomach.

"Oh, that helps," Estle said after a sip of his own.

"Jesus, I never knew it could get this cold," Clint said.

"I guess we're lucky we don't have to go through the mountains," the gambler said.

Clint shivered at the thought and tried to draw his coat closer around him.

"Don't even think it," Clint said, but then he was the one who was starting to think about it, as an idea began to form in his mind. He would have to think it through a little further before taking it up with Chooka.

When they finished eating they sat back with a cup of coffee each in their hands, enjoying the warmth it created, inside and out.

"If you're not wanted by the law," Clint asked, "what will you do when we get to Canada?"

"I don't know," Estle said. "I guess I'll cross over back into the United States and steer clear of Wyoming."

"Well, that leaves you plenty of other places to go."

"Maybe San Francisco," Estle said. "Have you ever been to San Francisco?"

"Oh, yes," Clint said, recalling that San Francisco was where this whole thing had started. "I just may have been to San Francisco one time too often."

"That's the place for a gambler," Estle said, as if he hadn't heard Clint's comment.

Estle had a dreamy look in his eyes, and Clint said, "Why don't you go to sleep and maybe you'll dream about it. I'll take the first watch."

"I won't argue with you," Estle said, finishing his coffee. "I just hope you don't wake me up in the middle of a pat hand."

"I'll try not to wake you while you have a smile on your face," Clint said.

"The hell with that," Estle replied. "That'll just mean I'm with a woman. Don't wake me while I have my poker face on!"

TWENTY-THREE

After an hour had gone by on his watch, Clint decided to try to engage Chooka in conversation. He poured a cup of coffee and carried it over to where the Indian was seated.

"Chooka?"

"Yes?" the Indian answered right away.

"Are you asleep?"

"A foolish question," the Indian said. "I was, but I am not now."

"Would you like a cup of coffee? It's getting pretty cold," Clint said.

"No," the Indian said. "My chilkat is all I need against the cold. You drink your coffee."

"Do you mind if I drink it here?"

"I do not."

Clint sat beside the Indian and sipped his coffee.

"You speak excellent English," he commented.

"Yes."

"Where did you learn?"

"In my village," Chooka said. He did not seem to be offended by Clint's questions and answered them quite readily. "A white holy man came and taught me."

"A priest?"

"Yes."

"That must have been a long time ago."

"Yes."

"While the Russians still owned Alaska?"

"Yes."

"Was the priest a Russian?"

"No."

Though he answered the questions readily, the Indian did not seem to be inclined to elaborate.

"Where was the priest from?"

"Your country."

"The United States?"

"Yes."

Probably a missionary, Clint thought. Looking at Chooka's face in the moonlight, and recalling what he had seen in daylight, he was unable to estimate the Indian's age. He could have been twenty-five or forty-five, or perhaps even older. The mustache and beard—*Odd on an Indian*, he thought again—made it even harder to guess. Being unable to guess Chooka's age made it just as hard to guess how long ago he might have learned English. The Russians sold Alaska in 1867, so it had to be before then.

"What were you doing in Cordova?"

"Passing through."

"Do you know Mallerby?"

"Who?"

"The man who arranged for you to be my guide."

"No."

"How did he know you, then?"

The Indian shrugged.

"Have you worked as a guide before?"

"Many times."

"Then you know more of Alaska than just the northern part, where you're from."

"Yes."

Clint was getting frustrated. He had a feeling that this was

Chooka's way of discouraging questions without seeming to.
It was working.

He decided to try a different tack, and ask about the idea
that had occurred to him earlier.

"Chooka, how could we arrive at Northway before someone leaving Glenallen did?"

For the first time the Indian looked at him, his eyes flat,
dark and expressionless. "From where?"

"From, say, Copper Center," Clint said.

The Indian looked away and said, "Over the mountains."

"Instead of around them."

"Yes."

"That would save us time and get us to Northway first?"
Clint asked.

Chooka hesitated, then said, "It is possible."

"But?"

The Indian did not respond.

"You don't sound too sure, Chooka," Clint said.
"What's the problem?"

"The way over the mountain is treacherous," the guide
answered.

"What would we need?"

"Good horses—"

"We have them."

"—a good guide—"

"We have that, too."

"—protection from the cold—"

"We could get that in Copper Center . . . couldn't we?"
Clint asked.

The Indian nodded.

"Then there's no problem," Clint said. "After we reach
Copper Center and get more supplies, we'll start over the
mountains."

Chooka looked at Clint, then looked behind him at the sleeping form of Estle, and then back to Clint.

He had asked a question without speaking a word, and what worried Clint—just a little—was that he understood it.

"Whether he comes with us or not will be up to him," Clint said. "I'll explain what we're going to do tomorrow, and he can make his decision by the time we reach Copper Center."

The Indian nodded, and stared into the dark. His eyes were open, but Clint had the distinct impression that were he to speak, the Indian would no longer hear him.

He decided not to test his theory. Instead, he got up and went back to the fire to start a new pot of coffee. In the moonlight he was able to look at the far off mountains, and shivered as he thought about how cold it must be up there.

He hoped Copper Center had some pretty heavy coats for sale—or maybe even some chilkats.

TWENTY-FOUR

They made Copper Center by midday, as Chooka had promised. It was decided—actually, suggested, by Chooka—that they spend the night in town and start off the following morning, especially if Clint was still determined to go over the mountains to Northway.

"I am," Clint told Chooka.

Chooka looked over at Estle, and Clint said, "I haven't told him yet. I'll let you know if there will be two of us or three of us, and you can buy provisions accordingly."

The Indian nodded and, having already handed his horse over to the livery man, went off on his own. They would meet later by the saloon.

Clint and Estle walked their horses into the livery themselves, and while they were unsaddling them Clint broached the subject of the trip over the mountains.

"You're crazy," Estle said.

"You don't have to come along, L.D.," Clint reminded Estle. "We're not joined at the hip or anything."

"I know that, but the mountains, Clint? Jesus Christ, man, it's freezing up there."

"It'll get me to Northway, hopefully first."

"With the head start your man must have on you, what makes you think he isn't already in Canada and gone?"

Clint told Estle about Mallerby's telegrams.

99

"That doesn't sound right to me," the gambler said.

"What doesn't?"

"Why would a man on the run move so slowly?"

Clint had wondered about that himself, though only in the back of his mind, and said so.

"Well, before you go through with your plan, you'd better think about it," Estle suggested.

"All right, but you think about it too," Clint said. "I don't mind telling you I could use the company. I tried having a conversation with Chooka last night during my watch."

"And?"

"He said about ten words."

"Yeah, I know," Estle said. "I tried it one night myself."

They finally turned their horses over to the liveryman to be cared for, and started for the hotel. They would each get a room, and then go over to the saloon for a cold beer.

Copper Center was indeed a mining town, and as such had a fairly large population crammed in a small area.

At the hotel Clint told the clerk they wanted two rooms and the clerk shook his head.

"Can't help you," he said. "Only got one."

"Is there anyplace else in town?"

"Sure," the clerk said, "a couple of rooming houses, but they ain't even got one room."

Clint and Estle looked at each other, and then Clint said, "What do you say?"

"What choice do we have?"

"We'll take it," Clint said.

"Have to charge you double."

"What?" Estle asked.

"House rule," the clerk said, shrugging. "If you don't want it, somebody else will."

"We'll take it," Clint said again.

The clerk pushed the registration book across the desk and Clint signed it, then turned the pen over to Estle.

"Why don't you let me take the gear up," Clint said, "and I'll meet you at the saloon."

"Fine with me," Estle said. "Just don't cry about me having a head start."

"Just don't order me a beer," Clint said. "I'll order it when I get there. I want a cold one . . . and then a hot cup of coffee."

"See you later."

Clint accepted Estle's saddlebags and rifle, then carried both their gear up to their room, which was barely big enough to accommodate the single bed. One of them would have to stretch out on the floor, which was almost as cold as the ground they'd been sleeping on for the past couple of days.

Clint dropped the gear on the bed, set the rifles down against the wall and started to leave the room. He stopped short at the door, turned and looked at the gear on the bed. He was considering going through Estle's gear, and then wondered what had given him the thought. Certainly the gambler had given him no reason to suspect him of anything.

Clint shook off the idea and left the hotel room, but all the way to the saloon it nagged at the back of his mind that maybe he should have looked. When he entered, however, he forgot all about it.

Until later.

TWENTY-FIVE

"Where do you suppose Chooka is going to sleep to-night?" Estle asked Clint. The gambler was working on his second beer while Clint drank his first.

"Who knows?" Clint said. "With no rooms available, do you want to share our closet with him?"

"I'm not that concerned," Estle hastened to point out.

After the beers were done, Clint suggested that they go and find a pair of gloves for Estle, and then find that cup of coffee he had mentioned.

"Or better yet," he added, "a pot."

"Maybe we'll even find another Wilma Sue," Estle added, hopefully.

"How many of those do you think there are?" Clint asked.

They found a store that specialized in mining supplies and Estle found a pair of gloves that, although a bit bulky for playing cards or handling a gun, would keep his hands warm.

"Even in the mountains," the storekeeper said, causing Clint and the gambler to exchange glances.

"Thanks," Estle said, paying for the gloves.

"Where can we get a good cup of coffee?" Clint asked.

"Go out the door to the left, down a couple of blocks," the storekeeper said. "Ain't no sign outside, but the place is called Dinah's. Best coffee in town."

"Thanks."

Outside Estle tried on his gloves and said, "Hell, that feels better already."

Clint did not have his gloves on, because that was a quick way for a man who has a rep with a gun to get himself killed. The Gunsmith knew of a few men who preferred to handle their guns with gloves on, but he preferred to be able to "feel" the gun.

"This must be it," Estle said.

"Crowded," Clint commented, looking in the window.

"See any Wilma Sues?"

"No, but I smell strong coffee," Clint said. "Come on, let's go inside and see if we can find a table."

As they entered Dinah's they were pleased to discover how warm it was inside. Estle took off his new gloves and shoved them inside his belt as they looked around for a table.

"Well, lookee there," Estle said. Over in a corner two men were getting up, so Clint and Estle walked over to claim the table.

"Hold it," one of the men said to them as they moved to sit down.

"You talking to us?" Estle asked.

"You don't work for the Billings mine," the man said.

"Good guess," Clint said, and sat down.

"You can't sit here," the second man said.

"Who says?" Estle asked, taking the other seat.

"This table is for the Billings mine only," the first man said.

"Is there a problem here?" a waitress asked, approaching with apprehension.

She was a handsome woman in her early forties, with long blond hair streaked with gray, and pleasant blue eyes. Her figure was trim, with a full bust that did not escape the notice of either Clint or Estle, in spite of the tension of the situation.

"These gentlemen are telling us that we can't sit here," Clint said.

"That's nonsense," she said.

"Dinah, you know this is our table—" the first man began, but she cut him right off.

"That's nonsense, Dave," she said. "My tables are open to anyone. This happens to be your men's favorite table, but I can't help that."

"Be hell to pay if any of our men come in here while these two are sitting here," the second man warned.

"There'd be hell to pay, all right," she said, "because if any of your men start trouble, I'll send for the sheriff."

"The sheriff works for Mr. Billings, Dinah," one of the men said.

"Well, he's supposed to work for the town," she said. "Now why don't you two get out of here and let me serve my customers."

The two men exchanged glances, then shrugged at each other. One threw Clint a dirty look, while the other sent one Estle's way, and then they left.

"What can I get you fellas?" the woman asked.

"We were told you had the best coffee in town," Clint said. "We'd like to start with that."

"Sure," she said. "Large pot or small?"

"Large, thank you."

"My pleasure," she said, smiling specifically for Clint's benefit.

As she walked away, hips swaying, Clint said, "You know, I'm all for the charms of young girls like Wilma Sue, but there's something to be said for a mature, experienced woman, as well."

"I can't argue with that."

When she returned she was carrying a tray with a large pot of coffee on it, and two cups. Well, actually, she set a cup down in front of Estle, and a larger mug down in front of the Gunsmith.

"You look like a man who enjoys a healthy cup of coffee," she said, pouring for him.

"You're right about that, ma'am," he said.

"Dinah," she told him, standing up straight.

"Dinah," he said. "My name's Clint Adams. This is my friend, L.D. Estle."

"Pleased to meet you," she said to L.D., but her eyes never left Clint. "Just passing through?"

"Yes, ma'am."

"Well, Copper Center hasn't got that much to recommend it, if you're not a miner," she said.

Clint tasted her coffee, which was extraordinary, and said, "Well, this coffee could sure keep a man here longer than he intended."

"That's very nice of you," she said. "Excuse me, but I have other customers."

"Of course."

When she left, Estle said, "Am I here, or am I imagining I'm here?"

"She just appreciates the charms of an older man, that's all," Clint told his younger friend.

"I'll say."

Estle tasted the coffee and said, "God, that's strong."

"That's the way I like it."

"You want to get something to eat?" the gambler asked. "It's pretty warm in here."

"Why not?" Clint said, watching Dinah move around the room. "The place has a certain charm."

Looking around the room Estle said, "This is the way business should be for Wilma Sue."

"I agree."

When Dinah looked their way Clint called her over and she responded promptly. "What can I do for you?"

"We'd like something to eat," he said. "Do you have a specialty?"

"I sure do," she said.

"Bring us two."

"All right—" she started to say, but when the door opened and four men stepped in, she frowned.

"Is something wrong?" Clint asked.

"Maybe," she said. "Those men are from the Billings mine."

"Is that so?"

"Maybe you'd better wait a few moments before ordering," she suggested.

"I think we'll have our order now, thanks," Clint said.

"I think I'd better send for the sheriff," she said and hurried away to fill their order, send for the sheriff, or both.

Clint was seated facing the door, so he had a clear view of the four miners.

"Are they looking our way?" Estle asked, without turning to see for himself.

"They are."

"Are they coming over?"

"They are."

Estle closed his eyes and said, "Are we in trouble again?"

Clint sighed and said, "I guess we are."

TWENTY-SIX

None of the four men who approached them were the two who had previously sat at the table, but they were all rather large fellows, as miners are apt to be.

"Can we help you?" Clint said, as the four men stopped by the table. Clint wanted to make sure he got the first word in.

"You fellas are sittin' at our table," one of the men said.

"Are you kidding?" Estle said. "This table wouldn't even fit the four of you."

"We'll fit," the man said, "as soon as you get up and leave."

"We'll get up and leave," Clint said, "after we've finished eating, and drinking our coffee."

"I don't think you understand," the spokesman said. "This is our table."

Clint remained silent and picked up his coffee cup left-handed to take a sip. His right hand was out of sight under the table.

"Look, mister," the man said, "we don't want no trouble, we just want our table. We just finished our shift and we're hungry."

"And dirty," Estle pointed out, wrinkling his nose at the smell the four miners were giving off.

"Another table should be opening up pretty soon," Clint said. "Why don't you just wait?"

"We don't want to wait," the man said. "If you and your friend don't move, we're just gonna have to move you ourselves."

"That wouldn't be advisable," Clint said.

"Why not?"

"Because I've got my gun out underneath this table," Clint said, "and if you make a move I don't like, I'm going to put a hole in your belly you could put your fist through."

The man blinked several times and seemed to take several mental steps backward.

"None of us are armed," he said, pointing out the obvious.

"That might give you some idea of how much I'm enjoying this coffee," Clint said.

The four men looked at each other with puzzled frowns, and then the spokesman asked, "Mister, are you gonna make us go get our guns?"

"Not unless you want to die over a table," Clint said.

Now all four men blinked as they realized that the seated man meant what he said.

"Mister," the spokesman said, almost apologetically, "I hope we don't ever catch you without your gun."

"You won't."

And I've got one too," Estle said. He opened his palm and showed them the derringer. "See?"

The spokesman shook his head sadly, and he and the other three turned around and walked out.

"Hell," Estle said, tucking the little gun back up his sleeve, "you scared the shit out of me."

Clint looked across the table at the gambler and then brought his right hand out from beneath the table, empty.

"Bluffing?" Estle said.

"I hate killing, L.D.," Clint said, "and I'd never do it over a table."

"Jesus," Estle said, shaking his head, "and I had my gun out."

Clint shrugged and sipped his coffee.

"With a poker face like that," Estle commented, "I don't think I'll ever play poker against you again."

A few minutes later, as Dinah was walking to their table with their order, the front door opened and a man with a badge pinned to his shirt walked in. He looked around, spotted Dinah, and walked over.

"Dinah, you sent someone to get me?" he asked.

She put the tray down on their table and turned to face the lawman with her hands on her hips.

"Yes, I did, but apparently I made a mistake in mentioning that I needed you because some of the Billings crew was starting trouble."

"What does that mean?" the lawman asked. He was in his early fifties, it seemed, with a nicotine-stained bushy mustache, and a worn Navy Colt on his hip.

"I guess what they say is true, Sheriff," she said. "Billings does own you."

"There's no call for you to talk that way, Dinah," the sheriff said. "I came because I heard there was trouble."

"Well, there isn't any trouble anymore, so you can just go back to doing whatever you were doing," Dinah said. She pointedly ignored the lawman then and began to remove plates from the tray and set them in front of Clint and Estle. The lawman stood there a few moments longer, then started to feel silly and resented Clint and Estle for having witnessed it. He glared at them, and left.

"Useless old fool," Dinah said under her breath. She leaned past Clint to set down a piece of apple pie he hadn't ordered, and brushed his shoulder firmly with her right breast.

"You handled him very well," Clint complimented.

"Thanks," she said, standing up straight and wiping her hands on her apron. "I'd like to thank you for handling the Billings boys without busting up my place."

"No problem," Clint said. "They didn't really want any trouble, anyway."

"Enjoy your meal," she told Clint. "Call if you need anything else."

"I will," he promised. She gave him a warm smile and went off to tend to the rest of her customers.

"What do you suppose she meant by 'anything'?" Estle asked, leaning over the table.

"If I had a mind like yours, I'd give it away," Clint said. "Sure."

Both men moved their plates around, preparing to start eating. Dinah's specialty was some kind of a meat and vegetable stew, and hunks of bread set in the center of the table were obviously meant to be used to soak up the gravy.

"Looks good," Clint said.

Estle picked up his fork, speared a piece of meat and fed it into his mouth. He chewed two or three times, then made a face and said, "If I had known it was going to taste like this, I would have given those four miners the table."

"It can't be that bad," Clint said. Under Estle's watchful eye Clint picked up a piece of meat and put it in his mouth. After a few seconds, he reached for his coffee mug and took a healthy swig.

"Well," he said, "at least the coffee's good."

TWENTY-SEVEN

The next morning Clint Adams woke up in Dinah's bed, in her room above the restaurant. He had spent much of the time after dinner watching Estle play poker, but the promise in Dinah's eyes—and words—had brought him back to her place later that night, and he was gratified to find that she was waiting for him.

She had taken him by the hand, locked the front doors of her place, and led him upstairs to her room, where she hastily removed her clothing, revealing to him her pale, firm breasts with their pink, budding tips.

"I haven't had time to bathe," she had said.

"In the morning," he'd said, "we'll both bathe."

He'd removed his clothes, and they had tumbled to the bed together. She had attacked him the way a thirsty man would attack a watering hole after walking through the desert. Apparently it had been a long time since she'd last found a man she wanted to be with.

What Clint had told Estle earlier was proven that night to be true. There was nothing like an experienced woman.

Dinah had rolled him onto his back and covered his body with moist kisses, working her way down until she had his erect cock firmly planted in both hands. She'd laved the swollen tip with her tongue, then released her hold on him so that her tongue could travel the length of his shaft. Finally, she had captured him in her mouth, taking a surprising

113

amount of him, and sucked at him until he filled her mouth with his seed, which she hungrily swallowed.

After that she had again used her mouth to bring him to fullness, then straddled him and impaled herself on his hard rod. She rode him the way a man might ride an unbroken horse, and their subsequent couplings throughout the night were just as violent—and satisfying.

Now, with the sun almost up, he put his hand on her back and shook her gently.

"I'm awake," she said.

"I have to go."

"I know," she said. "I would rather you left while I was asleep, but once I woke up I couldn't get back to sleep." She sat up in bed, her full breasts swaying slightly, slapping together. "Do you want that bath?"

"No time," he said. "Maybe just a basin . . ."

"I'll get it."

She stood up and pulled on a high-collared dress, then went out to get him the water basin. When she returned he was dressed except for his shirt. He used the water to wash his face, neck and chest, then dried off and put on his shirt.

"Thank you," she said, putting her arms around his waist. "I'd almost forgotten what it was like."

She was a sad woman, he had discovered during the night, and he was sorry if his leaving would make her sadder, but there was nothing he could do about that.

"Maybe you'll come back this way," she said, stepping back.

"Maybe," he said, pulling on his coat, but they both knew that he would not.

"Good-bye, Dinah," he said to her, and as he left her room, he realized that he had never gotten around to asking her what her last name was.

TWENTY-EIGHT

Before leaving the saloon the previous night, Clint had gotten Estle's answer about accompanying him on the mountain trip.

"Yes," Estle had said, "if you're sure you want to go through with it."

"I'm sure I haven't got much choice," Clint had said. He had given Estle money to give Chooka, so that the Indian guide could buy the necessary supplies.

"Just tell him not to buy so much that we need a pack horse," he'd said. "We have three horses between us, so we should be able to carry enough provisions."

When he reached the livery that morning, both Chooka and Estle were there waiting for him.

"Got the supplies?" he asked.

"We've got them," Estle said.

"Let's get saddled up, then," he said.

Chooka was already sitting astride his horse, so he waited patiently while Clint and Estle mounted up. They divided the provisions evenly, and everything fit in their saddlebags, with an extra canvas sack each.

"What are these?" Clint asked, holding up two blankets.

"Chooka bought them for us," Estle said, taking one. "He says they're not chilkats, but they should help fight the cold at night."

115

"Anything that'll help," Clint said, tying the blanket to the back of Duke's saddle.

"How was your night?" Estle asked.

"A hell of a lot better than our dinner," Clint said. "What happened at the hotel?"

"I convinced the clerk that I shouldn't pay double, since you'd found another place to stay. He wasn't happy, but he saw it my way."

"Glad to hear it," Clint said, cinching Duke's saddle up tight. "We'll split the cost, anyway."

"No need," Estle assured him. "I had a very good night at the saloon."

"I never doubted that you wouldn't," Clint said. "You ready?"

"I'm ready."

They rode outside, paid the livery man what they owed him, and then Clint said, "All right, Chooka. Lead on."

"The way through the mountains is very hard," the Indian reminded him.

"I know that," Clint said, "but we've got to get to Northway as soon as possible."

The Indian shrugged, and led the way.

"Clint," Estle said, as they followed.

"What?"

"What if the man you're looking for also took the mountain route?"

"Then he's farther ahead of us than I thought," Clint said. "It would explain why he hadn't reached Glenallen when Mallerby sent his telegram."

"It would, yeah," Clint agreed, "but why take unnecessary chances? He's traveling unfamiliar territory as it is."

"You can't assume that," Estle said. "What if he's been in Alaska before? What if he also hired a guide?"

"Why do you have to be so optimistic all the time?" Clint

asked Estle sarcastically. "Do you have a better idea, L.D.?"

Estle paused a moment, then said, "Well, no, actually, I can't say that I do."

"Then what do you say you stop trying to cheer me up all the time, and we'll get on with our trip?"

"You're the boss," Estle said. "I'm just along for the ride."

TWENTY-NINE

The Gunsmith had to admit one thing when he, Estle, and Chooka finally rode into Northway, Canada—tired, hungry, cold and sore—and that was that Chooka had taken damned good care of all of them—men and horses.

During the past few days the guide had babied them, taught them how, when and where to sleep in the mountains, in order to minimize the effect of the numbing cold.

"Sometimes," Chooka had said, at one point, "you could go to sleep and just never wake up—unless you know how."

Clint had been able to believe that. Even in their blankets, the cold had cut into them like a sharp knife. Chooka, in his chilkat, hadn't even seemed to feel it.

He had also taught them when and how much to eat, and when to walk and ride their horses. The horses, in fact, had passed over that mountain with little or no wear and tear, because Chooka had looked out for them every step of the way. He had treated the horses better than he treated the men—including himself—and with good reason. Without those animals, they never would have made it.

As they pulled their horses to a stop in front of the Northway livery stable, Estle said, "My God, that Indian did it. I thought we'd freeze solid on that mountain, but he got us through."

"That's what he was being paid to do," Clint said, stretch-

119

ing in the saddle. "My God, I don't think I've ever been as bone weary as I am right now."

"That mountain pass he said nobody knew about," Estle said. "I still don't know about it. It was barely big enough for us to squeeze through."

Clint dismounted, and Estle followed. Chooka gave his horse to the liveryman, and as before, Clint and Estle walked their own mounts in and unsaddled them.

"I'm going over to the hotel," Estle said.

"You go ahead," Clint said. "I'll be along. I want to make sure Duke is settled in all right."

"Want me to check you in?"

"Only if they haven't got enough rooms," Clint said. "Otherwise I'll take care of it myself."

"All right," Estle said, and he dragged himself out of the stable and over to the hotel.

Clint took care to rub Duke down good, and make sure he had enough feed.

"We had a rough trip, didn't we, big boy?" Clint said. "Of course, you came through real well, just like I knew you would."

Duke nodded his big head, and looked at Clint as if to say, You came through it pretty well, yourself.

"You relax, big fella," Clint said, patting Duke's massive neck. "You earned some time to relax . . . and hell, so have I."

Clint picked up his gear and walked over to the Northway Hotel. Northway was not a mining town, and although it wasn't much larger than Copper Center, the hotel had plenty of rooms.

"You got bath facilities?" he asked.

" 'Round back," the clerk said.

"I'm going to put my gear in my room," Clint said. "Could you have a hot bath drawn for me?"

"That'll be twenty-five cents."

Clint paid the two bits and then went up to his room. It wasn't much larger than the one in Copper Center, but at least he didn't have to share it—not that he had actually shared the other one, but that was beside the point.

Clint carried his gunbelt and some clean clothes downstairs with him, where he found his hot bath waiting. He locked the door, moved a chair over by the tub and hung the gunbelt on the back of it, within easy reach, then lowered himself into the steaming hot water inch by inch. Once he was settled in, he closed his eyes and allowed the hot water to bake the aches out of his joints.

With any kind of luck at all, he should be able to sit back now and wait for Paul Martel to come riding into his arm. That's if he hadn't gone north, and if he wasn't already in Canada.

Clint stared tiredly at the ceiling, wondering how his friend West was doing, wondering if all of this effort was worth it—and then he thought about how he'd had Paul Martel in custody, and had just let him go, to spite Fenton for lying to him.

There was a decision that had come back to haunt him, all right.

When the water started to get tepid—and had changed color to a murky brown—he lifted himself out of the tub and dried himself off. He put on his fresh clothes, strapped on his gun, and left the hotel in search of a cup of coffee.

In looking for a café, Clint happened to pass the sheriff's office. In Cordova, and in Copper Center, he had not followed his usual policy of checking in with the local law. He did not want to announce his arrival to anyone, just in case Paul Martel was around. This time he decided to stop in and check with the local law. The sheriff had to be the one who would have received a telegram from Mallerby, checking to see if Paul Martel had passed through Northway yet, so he shouldn't be surprised when, five or six days later, Clint asked the same question.

He opened the door to the sheriff's office and walked in. The sheriff was seated at his desk, and looked up as Clint entered.

"Hello, Sheriff," he said.

"Hello," the lawman replied, looking at Clint curiously. "What can I do for you?"

"My name's Clint Adams, Sheriff."

"Sheriff Walt Pulley."

"I'm following up a telegram you received from Cordova five or six days ago," Clint said.

"A telegram?"

"Yes, from John Mallerby, assistant to the military commander," Clint said.

The sheriff frowned. "I don't remember any such telegram, Mr. Adams."

Clint tried again. "It was asking if a man named Paul Martel had passed through Northway."

"I'm sorry," the sheriff said, shaking his head, "but I received no such telegram."

Clint stood stunned, staring at the sheriff in disbelief. Mallerby said he had sent the telegram. Had he skipped Northway? If he had, it had not been a smart move, on his part.

"You do have a telegraph office, don't you?"

"Yes, we do, but as I said—"

"Let me ask you now, then," Clint said, interrupting the lawman before he could go any further. "Have you ever heard of a man named Paul Martel?"

"I have not."

"Do you keep track of all the strangers who pass through town?"

"Whenever possible," the lawman said. "I appreciate your coming here—"

"Perhaps you'd remember him if I described him," Clint said, and proceeded to do so.

"I have seen no such man," the sheriff said, "but I am getting very curious about this. Just what is your business?"

Clint barely heard the question, and when the sheriff repeated it, he said, "I'm just a gunsmith, Sheriff. That's all, just a gunsmith."

THIRTY

Clint obtained directions from the sheriff to two places: a café with good coffee, and the telegraph office. He left the lawman's office with the intention of going first to the telegraph office, but he came upon the café and went inside.

It was midafternoon, and the place was empty.

"What can I get you, sir?" the waitress asked. He looked up at her, saw a woman in her early fifties, whose best days were way, way behind her. No Wilma Sue, and no Dinah, that was for sure.

"Just coffee," he said.

"A cup of coffee," she said, but as she turned away he stopped her.

"A pot of coffee, not a cup," he said.

"A pot," she said, and went off to get it.

Clint rested his elbows on the table and pondered what he had learned from Sheriff Pulley. No telegram had been sent from John Mallerby asking about Paul Martel. There could only be two reasons for that. One: Mallerby did not think that Martel could have gotten that far, and only sent his telegrams as far as Glenallen. Bad judgment on Mallerby's part, but that was all he could be faulted for. On the other hand, if Mallerby was in Martel's pocket—if John Mallerby even existed—then the only telegram he would have sent would have been to Martel.

Which meant Martel was waiting somewhere for the

Gunsmith—but where? Glenallen? That made sense. Mallerby had told Clint that Martel had not yet reached Glenallen. He was trying to send Clint there and Clint had unwittingly double-crossed him. If that was true, then he was ahead of Martel, not behind him.

This may have turned out better than he expected, in spite of Mallerby's efforts.

And what about Chooka? If Mallerby was a phony, what about the Indian?

When the coffee came, Clint took his time over it, deciding what his next move should be. He couldn't trust anything Mallerby had said, not until he checked with Glenallen and Copper Center to see if telegrams had been sent there.

What about confiding in Estle? If he couldn't trust Mallerby, and Chooka, could he trust the gambler?

When the coffeepot was empty, he headed for the telegraph station where he sent off telegrams, carefully worded, to the sheriffs of Copper Center and Glenallen, with references of his own, so that they wouldn't reroute his requests through the office of the military commander.

"When an answer comes in, I'll be at the saloon," he told the young clerk.

"Want me to wait for both?"

He gave the clerk four bits and said, "I want each answer when it comes in, son—on the double."

"Yes, sir!"

Clint walked over to the saloon, where he found Estle already involved in a poker game. He gave a little wave of acknowledgment and walked to the bar.

"Beer," he said, watching Estle in the mirror.

Now he knew that he should have checked the gambler's gear that day in Copper Center. It might have allayed any questions that were going through his head right now.

"Thanks," he said when the bartender brought him the

beer. He sipped the cold beer and continued to study Estle through the mirror.

L.D. had given no indication of being anything but what he said, a gambler. There was only one way to find out if he was anything else, and that meant going back to the telegraph office and sending some telegrams to friends who were still wearing badges.

He finished his beer, brushed off a couple of girls, waved to Estle and left. The gambler frowned at Clint's back as the Gunsmith walked out of the saloon, but quickly became caught up in his card game once again.

"No answer yet, mister," the boy said as he walked back into the office.

"I'm not worried about that," he said. "I want to send a few more telegrams."

"Well, go ahead."

He gave the boy a dollar and said, "And I don't want anyone to know about them."

"Yes, sir!"

Clint sent out three telegrams, and then decided to send a fourth to San Francisco. It was worded so that no one but Fenton would understand what it meant. He figured to be in Northway for at least a day, long enough for Fenton to get word to him on West's condition.

Maybe longer.

Maybe long enough for word to get to Martel. Knowing that it was the Gunsmith might cause Martel to run, but Clint didn't think so. He had cost Martel a lot the first time they met.

Martel wouldn't run.

THIRTY-ONE

The next day, Clint Adams met Joanna Morgan, and his life changed.

THIRTY-TWO

The next morning Clint asked the desk clerk at the Northway restaurant where the best breakfast in town was to be had.

"There's a café on the side street," the clerk said. "Street ain't got no name, but the place is behind the general store. Follow your nose."

"I'll follow it," he said. "Thanks."

"Your friend already left."

Clint was turning to leave, and stopped. "My friend?"

"The one with the funny name," the clerk said. "The gambler."

"How do you know he's a gambler?"

The clerk had to be nearly seventy years old. His skin was wrinkled and discolored, but his eyes sparkled, a bright blue, wise and alert.

"I know a gambler when I see one, son."

"And me?"

"A gambler," the old man said, "but of a different sort. You don't gamble with cards."

"What do I gamble with?"

"That," the old man said, indicating his gun, "and with your life. So far you're a winner, son."

"Everybody's got to lose sometime, old-timer," Clint said.

131

"Ain't that the bitchin' truth."

"Did you send my friend over there for breakfast?"

"Nope."

"Why not?"

"He didn't ask," the old man answered, cackling, "but I don't think I'd've sent him there, anyway—and don't ask me why. You I cotton to, but your young friend, I don't."

"Are you a good judge of character, old-timer?"

"Fair to middlin'," the man answered, "but I could change my mind about you, if'n you call me old-timer one more time."

"What should I call you, then?"

"Morgan," the man said. "That's my last name."

"What's your first name?"

"That's a question I don't never answer," the old man said. "I don't like being called by my first name," he added, "jest like you don't like being called the Gunsmith."

Clint, ready to leave, walked back to the desk now, eyeing Morgan with interest. "How'd you know that?"

"I seen you," the old man said, "in Abilene. You and Ol' Jim Hickok."

"I see you?" Clint asked.

"Nah," he said. "I was passin' through. Fact is, that's the last time I set a horse. Ain't set nothing but this desk since I got here."

"You and me should have a drink, Morgan," Clint said.

"Whenever yer ready, lad," Morgan said. "Now why don't you go on over and have yer breakfast. You'll see my daughter over there."

"Your daughter?"

"Joanna. Big gal with red hair, like mine used to be—when I still had some," he said, running his frail hand over his liver-spotted dome. "Good-looking gal too, like her mother. You tell her I said to make sure you eat right."

Clint grinned and said, "I'll tell her, ol—Morgan."

The old man cackled, and Clint turned and left the hotel.

Clint found the place Morgan had been talking about easy enough, and once inside found his daughter even easier. The old man had been telling the truth.

Joanna Morgan was a big redhead, even sitting down. She had a green ribbon tied in her hair, and her eyes were green. She reminded Clint uncomfortably of another red-haired woman in his past, Jenny Sand,* but if it was possible, Joanna was even lovelier than Jenny had been. Joanna appeared to be in her early thirties, and as Clint approached her table, she looked at him boldly.

"Can I help you," she said, "or do you just like to stare?"

"Well, ma'am," Clint said, "as worth staring at as you are, fact is your father sent me over from the hotel. I asked him where the best breakfast in town was to be had."

"Poppa sent you to the right place, mister."

"My name is Adams, Clint Adams," he said, "and he said I should tell you to make sure I ate right."

"Well," she replied, "I'm a dutiful daughter, if nothing else. Pull up a chair and I'll order for you."

"I appreciate it."

He sat opposite her as she called over a chubby young waitress and told her to "bring the gentleman the works."

"Do you like strong coffee?" she asked.

"As strong as I can get it."

"Try that, then," she said, indicating the pot on the table between them. "Use my cup."

She passed him her cup, then poured some coffee into it for him. He tasted it and found it to his liking.

"You're still staring," she said, smiling an amused smile.

"You remind me of someone," he said.

---

*The Gunsmith #2: The Chinese Gunman and #3: The Woman Hunt

"An old lover?" she asked, boldly.

"Yes."

"I don't know if I like that," she said.

The waitress came with an extra cup then, and Clint returned the favor and poured her a cup of coffee.

"Thank you," she said. "How do I remind you of her?"

"Your hair, your eyes," he said. "Same color."

"Was she beautiful?"

"Yes."

She looked closely at him, and then said, "She would have to be."

"But not as beautiful as you," he said.

"You know," she replied, "I believe you really mean that. Are you, by any chance, an honest man?"

"Why?"

"Because I would never become involved with a dishonest man," she said.

"In that case," he said, "I guess I'm an honest man."

She studied his face, still wearing the amused smile, and said, "Maybe I'll find out."

"Yep," he said, "maybe you will."

THIRTY-THREE

They spent the day together, much of it right there at that table. People came in for breakfast, left, came back for lunch, and Clint and Joanna were still there at the same table.

"I like your father," he said, as the afternoon wore on.

"He's a dear man," she said. "It kills him that he can't get out from behind that desk without help."

"We're supposed to have a drink together later."

"He must really like you then," she said.

"He—" he began, then stopped short.

"What?" she asked. "What is it?"

"He says he saw me, in Abilene, with Hickok," he said, watching her face for her reaction.

Her mouth formed a silent "oh," and then she said, "You're *that* Clint Adams."

"Yes."

"The Gunsmith?"

He made a face and said, "Yes."

"You don't like that name?"

"Not what it's come to mean," he told her. He explained to her how he felt about his reputation, what it had done to his life. He told her things in that one afternoon that he'd never told anyone else, some things that he'd never even told himself. It seemed that not only was he getting to know her better, but himself, as well.

"I imagine anyone who knows you wouldn't believe any of what's said, anyway," she said. "I know I don't, and I've only known you a few hours."

"A few hours can mean a lot," he said.

"Yes."

There was an awkward silence, and Clint broke it by asking, "What do you do here in town?"

"I used to be a schoolteacher," she said, "but when Poppa bought the hotel he wrote to me and asked me to come and help him run it, so here I am."

"Why did he settle here?"

"I don't know, really," she said. "I think he was just trying to see as much as he could before his legs gave out, and this is where he ended up."

"Why don't you take him back somewhere warm?" Clint asked. "Seems to me that would do his legs some good."

"Poppa doesn't want to move again," she said. "He's very old, and it wouldn't be an easy trip for him."

"I guess not."

"It's a shame you have to be stuck here though," Clint said.

"It's not so bad," she said.

Clint looked up then and noticed that the lunch crowd had long since cleared out.

"My God, we've been here a long time," he said.

"I guess we have," she agreed. "I've got to get back to the hotel and help Poppa."

"I've got some things to do as well," Clint said. They both stood up and Clint paid the bill. "You tell your father I'll be by later for that drink."

"I will."

"And maybe afterward, we could have dinner together?" he asked.

She smiled and said, "I'd like that, Clint."

"Good," he said. "Then I'll see you later."

Clint left to walk to the telegraph office. He couldn't believe that he had spent the entire morning talking to and confiding in a woman he had only just met. Hell, he'd slept with women on short acquaintance before, but never really talked to one.

This one was different, he told himself. It wasn't fair to compare her to Jenny Sand, or any of the other women in his past.

This one was different.

THIRTY-FOUR

When Clint walked into the telegraph office the young clerk smiled and waved three pieces of paper at him.

"You got three answers early today, mister, but you weren't in the saloon."

"It didn't occur to you to check the hotel huh?" Clint asked, taking the messages.

The clerk looked crestfallen, but Clint threw him two bits and said, "Forget it, just keep an ear out for the rest."

"Yes, sir!"

Two of the messages were from lawmen friends of his, and apparently Estle's story about being on the run from a woman and her family couldn't be verified. According to Clint's friends, Estle was not wanted by the law.

The third telegram was from San Francisco, written so only Clint would know what it said. West's condition was improving. Good news then, but still not the news that Clint really wanted. Why had these messages come in before the others, which were only sent to other towns in Alaska?

He stuffed the slips into his pocket and made for the saloon. Estle would be glad to hear that he wasn't wanted— by the law, that is.

As he had expected, Clint found Estle involved in a poker game. He got himself a beer and then walked over to the table.

"Afternoon," he greeted the gambler.

"You sleep late, partner," Estle said.

"I've been up," Clint said. He took out one message and passed it to the gambler. "Got a telegram I thought you might be interested in."

"About what?" He accepted the telegram and while somone else was dealing, read it. "Well, now . . ." He handed it back to Clint. "That's good news."

"It sure is," Clint said. "Congratulations."

"I'm much obliged, Clint," Estle said. "Now I can play this game with a free mind."

Clint looked at the pile of money in front of his friend and said, "Why don't they all just hand you their money?"

"No sport in that, Clint, no sport," Estle said, picking up his cards. Clint caught a glimpse of a hand full of hearts, and then retreated to the bar.

Much as he wanted to concentrate on Paul Martel, he found his thoughts turning towards Joanna Morgan. Clint's attitude toward women—especially after what had happened with Jenny Sand and later with Carolyn Gray Fox*—had been pretty cavalier. He'd sworn never to get so emotionally involved that he couldn't walk away. That was why he was so surprised at himself for his reaction to Joanna after only a few hours of conversation. He considered canceling their dinner engagement but thought that it might be better if he went and proved to himself that he could head off any kind of emotional involvement. Right now what he had to do was get her out of his thoughts so he could concentrate on business.

By the time Clint ordered a second beer, a boy came running into the saloon, looked around, picked him out, and approached him, holding out some telegrams.

"The man said you'd gimme two bits," the boy said, looking up at Clint boldly.

*The Gunsmith #17: Silver War

"Is that so?"

"Yep."

"Well the man was wrong," Clint said, and as the boy pulled back the hand holding the messages he added, " 'cause I'm going to give you four bits."

"Four bits?" the boy asked, wide-eyed. He couldn't have been more than eight or nine years old, and to him four bits was all the money in the world. *Hell*, Clint thought as he gave the kid the money, *four bits is all the money in the world to some grown men*.

"Take the money and run, kid," he said

"Thanks, mister!"

Clint leaned his elbows on the bar, with his beer between them, and read the telegrams. The one from Copper Center said the same as the one from Glenallen: Neither of their lawmen had received a telegram from a man named Mallerby about a man named Martel. Neither of them had ever heard of either man.

That clinched it, he thought, crumbling the telegrams into little yellow balls. He'd been sent on a wild goose chase, and Paul Martel could have been anywhere by now.

Anywhere at all.

THIRTY-FIVE

"How about that drink, Morgan?"

Clint entered the hotel lobby with a bottle of whiskey, and the old man behind the counter cackled happily.

"Sure thing, lad," he said. "We just got to get Joanna to come out here and take care of the desk. She's in the back."

Clint walked around the desk and stuck his head through the curtained doorway. Joanna was seated at a desk, going over what looked like the hotel accounts.

"Hi."

She looked up, then smiled and said, "Well, hello."

"Need a break from those numbers?"

"I sure do," she said. "No matter how hard I stare at them, they don't change."

She got up from her chair and Clint said, "Your Poppa and me want to have that drink."

She stared at him and said, "You look like you've had a few already."

"One or two," he admitted.

"Are you all right?"

"I'm just fine," he lied.

She continued to stare at him with concern, until he backed out of her eyesight.

"If you help me down from this stool," Morgan said, "I can hobble on back there."

Clint lifted the old man by the waist, and was shocked at how light and brittle he felt.

"Put me on my feet, damn it," the old man said, and Clint set him down.

The girl came out from the back and said, "Don't drink too much, Poppa."

"Why the hell not?" the old man demanded.

"You're not as young as you used to be," she said, with a grin.

"Ain't that the bitchin' truth," the old man said.

Clint followed the old man into the back room, where Morgan settled himself into a soft armchair.

"Pour me one of them right quick, lad," he said.

Clint poured a drink and handed it to him. Morgan took a sip, then leaned his head back and closed his eyes.

"This is the only time life's worth living anymore," he confided. "When I'm sitting in this chair with a drink in my hand."

"You've got a lovely daughter," Clint said, sitting behind the desk. The chair was still warm from Joanna. "That's worth living for, isn't it?"

"She'll be better off when I'm dead," the old man said. "She can go back where it's civilized, meet up with a good man and get married. A woman is meant to have kids, not take care of an old man who might as well be one."

"She doesn't seem to mind too much."

"She's a good girl, that's why," the old man said. He opened his eyes and fixed Clint with a watery look.

"She'd make a fine wife, lad," he said.

"I'm . . . not in the market," Clint said, pouring himself another drink.

"Hah!" the old man snapped. "Neither was I when I met her ma. I was about your age too as I recollect."

"Is that a fact?"

"Man's gotta have kids, lad," Morgan said. "Leave his mark in this world." The old man looked at Clint hard then and said, "But I guess you already left your mark, haven't you, Mr. Gunsmith?"

"Not the kind I'd like, Morgan," Clint said.

"There's something bothering you, son?" Morgan asked. "Something maybe I could help you with, or Joanna?"

"Not really," Clint said. "Nothing you could help with."

"What about Joanna?"

Clint hesitated, looked at the curtained doorway, and said, "She's a fine girl, Morgan, there's no doubt about that."

"Hah!" the old man said, slapping his knee and cackling. "I knew it."

"Knew what?"

"I knew you'd take to each other right off."

"That may be so, Morgan," Clint said, "but that doesn't mean that anything can ever come of it."

"Can if you want it to," the old man said, "sure enough can if you want it to."

"Have another drink, Morgan," Clint said, rising and pouring a little into the old man's glass.

"You call that a drink?" the old man asked sourly, examining the few drops in the bottom of his glass.

"We don't want Joanna getting mad at me, do we?" Clint asked. He went back and sat down behind the desk. "What do you want to talk about, Morgan?" Clint looked into his own glass. "Abilene? Hickok?"

"Let's talk about you, son," the old man answered.

"Me," Clint asked, "or the Gunsmith?"

"Just you, lad," Morgan said. "What's bothering you?"

"There're a couple things bothering me, Morgan," Clint said, leaning forward and lowering his voice, "only one of which is your daughter."

● ● ●

Clint left the old man dozing in his chair and went through the curtained doorway, behind the desk.

Joanna Morgan turned as she heard him and asked, "Is he all right?"

"He's fine," he told her. "He dozed off."

"Let him sleep, then," she said. "He doesn't sleep very well at night."

"His legs?"

She shook her head. "He has dreams. About the old days."

Clint knew what that was like, but he didn't say anything, he just nodded.

"What about you?" she asked. "Are you all right?"

"Me? I'm just fine."

She stared at him and said, "I don't believe that, but we can talk about it later."

"Yeah," he said, "later."

That's what he was afraid of. Find yourself a woman you can talk to, and you've found more problems than you can handle.

THIRTY-SIX

He went to his room to wash up and shake off the effects of some of the whiskey he'd been drinking. He put on a fresh change of clothes, strapped on his gun, then went downstairs to pick up Joanna for dinner. She was standing behind the desk with an older woman, giving her last minute instructions.

"Thank you for helping out, Mrs. Evans."

"Oh, that's no problem, dear," the woman said. "I have nothing else to do anyway," the woman went on, and when she saw Clint she added, "and you obviously have."

Joanna turned and smiled at Clint.

"Are you ready?" he asked.

"I haven't had time to change," she said.

"You look fine," he said. "You look beautiful."

"In that case, I guess I'm ready," she said. "Same place?"

"I don't care," he said. He wasn't thinking about food, he was just thinking about spending some more time with her.

They walked to the restaurant where they had met and had no trouble getting a table. The people who ran it seemed to know Joanna very well.

"They treat you pretty well here," he observed.

"The people who own this place came to town about the same time Poppa and I did. We got to be good friends."

It was a family business, and the chubby waitress was the daughter of the couple who owned the place.

"This is Lisa," Joanna said, introducing them. "Lisa, this is my friend, Clint Adams."

"Hi," Lisa said. She appeared to be about sixteen, and she would have been very pretty if she were able to lose some weight. "What can I get for you?"

Clint looked at Joanna, indicating that she should do the ordering. Joanna ordered two complete steak dinners, and a large pot of coffee.

"Do you want to tell me what's bothering you before dinner, or after?" Joanna asked after Lisa had gone to fill their order.

"Do I have a choice in the matter?"

"Just what I've given you," she said. "Before or after?"

"How about during?"

Clint outlined his problem for Joanna, without mentioning any names.

"So you're out in the middle of nowhere, with no idea of where he is, has been, or is headed," she summed up.

"That's it."

"What do you do next?"

"Give up?"

She stared at him and said, "Somehow that just doesn't sound right coming out of your mouth."

"Doesn't feel right either," he said, "but what else can I do?" he asked.

"So give up, then," she said. "But what do you feel so guilty about?"

At that point Lisa appeared carrying a tray bearing their food, and they suspended their conversation until she had served them and left.

"All right," she said, picking up where they had left off, "why do you feel guilty?"

"The would-be assassin is someone that I caught up with a few years ago and let go," Clint said. "If I hadn't let him go then, this wouldn't have happened."

"You must have had a good reason at the time," she said.

"I thought I did," he said, "but I'm not so sure anymore."

"Who did the man try to kill?"

"I can't tell you that, Joanna," he said.

"Somebody big, huh?" she asked.

"Big enough."

"Big as the President?"

Clint stopped eating and stared at her.

"What made you say that?"

She shrugged and said, "I don't know, but I guess that must be it, huh?"

"Close," he said, "very close."

"I guess the government figured they couldn't get a better man than the—" she stopped herself short, but Clint knew what she had been about to say.

"The Gunsmith, right?"

"Well, it just struck me that it had to be someone with a lot of money or power to get you to come all the way up here after someone," she said. "I didn't think you'd do it for money—"

"I've done a lot of things for money," he said, interrupting her.

"Maybe, but you wouldn't be feeling so guilty about this if it were just a matter of money. I figured it had to be a senator, or maybe the President himself."

"A logical conclusion based on an illogical assumption," he said. "You're making assumptions about me, and you don't even know me."

"Oh, I wouldn't say that," she said, cocking her head to one side and studying his face. "I think I know you pretty well, Mr. Clint Adams. And I'll tell you something else."

"What?"

"I think you're letting me get to know you, and you probably don't do that very often."

"You're right."

"So, why me?"

"I've been asking myself the same question since this morning," he answered. "I haven't come up with an answer yet."

"I know how you feel," she said.

"You do?"

"Mm-hm," she said, nodding. "I have the same urge, to open myself up to you, and I don't know why either."

Leaning forward Clint said, "Maybe we should help each other try and find out, Joanna."

"Maybe," she said. "Maybe we will—after dinner."

THIRTY-SEVEN

After dinner they went back to the hotel. Joanna looked in on her father, who was still sleeping in his chair, and asked Mrs. Evans if she could stay a little longer.

"Of course, dear," she said. "Let your father sleep."

Joanna turned to Clint and said, "I guess I'll see you tomorrow, then."

"Sure," he said. Joanna had her back to Mrs. Evans, and a secret grin on her face, because they both knew that Clint was going to his room, and that Joanna was going to use the back stairs to join him.

"Good night," she said. "Thanks for dinner."

"My pleasure."

When Clint started upstairs, Joanna was telling Mrs. Evans that she had some paperwork to do in her room, and would be down later on.

"No problem, child . . ." Clint heard, and then he was out of earshot.

He went to his room and removed his gunbelt, which he hung on the bedpost. He sat on the bed to remove his boots, and then stopped there. He was feeling things he had never felt before, and this confused him.

He was feeling anticipation, and that was normal, but he was also feeling nervous, and that definitely was not normal. He had never felt nervous about being with a woman before, not since the very first time. That was the only way to

151

describe it. He felt like a kid again, waiting for his first girl.

When her knock came on the door it was soft, almost hesitant. Was she feeling nervous as well? He'd never know unless he got up and let her in.

"I feel like a schoolgirl," she said, standing in the hall with her hands clasped in front of her.

"You'd better come in then before someone sees you," he said.

"I'm not ashamed of what we're going to do," she told him, but then she looked up and down the hall and said, "but I'd better hurry in, anyway."

She stepped past him and he closed the door.

"Somehow," she said, facing him, "I knew you'd still be dressed."

"I took my boots off," he argued, and then they both began to laugh.

"This is silly," she said.

"Is it?"

"I mean, we're acting like a couple of kids on our first night," she said.

"I had the same thought."

She came close to him and put her hands on his forearms.

"Maybe it's because we both know that this is more than a casual thing," she said.

"It can't be," he said. "Not after one day."

"You mean, you don't want it to be," she said.

"Joanna, I—"

"I'm not going to try and force you to say it, Clint," she said, beginning to unbutton his shirt, "but before we're through, you're going to feel it too."

She finished unbuttoning his shirt and slid her hands inside it, running her palms over his chest. Clint couldn't deny that he was excited just by the touch of her hands, by the feel of her breath on his face, by the closeness of her body to his. He put his arms around her and crushed her against him, and then two hungry mouths came together.

Joanna pulled the shirt off of Clint, and he pulled hers out of her pants. They parted long enough to divest themselves of the rest of their clothes, and then came together in another fiery embrace, mouths working avidly.

Her breasts were large and firm, and the hardened nipples dug into his chest. Her arms were wound tightly around him—as his were around her—and he was surprised by her strength.

Abruptly, she pushed him away and stood back. Her breasts were heaving as she tried to catch her breath, her nostrils were flaring and the look on her face was one of almost savage hunger.

"Oh, this is right," she told him, "this is so right, and don't try to tell me it isn't."

He advanced on her and she caught his hands and pulled him back to the bed. They went down with him on top, and she trapped his erection between her powerful thighs. He began to kiss and suck at her beautiful breasts and she moaned her approval, raking his back with her nails. His penis was still trapped between her thighs, and he reached down to force them apart so that he could drive himself into the steamy depths of her.

She brought her legs up and around his waist and he reached beneath her to cup her buttocks in his hand. In no time at all they found the proper rhythm, and then it was right for both of them—then, and through the remainder of their time together that night.

"I have to go back downstairs," she said later. She was lying within the circle of his arms, and although he tightened his hold on her, he said nothing.

"Mrs. Evans will be wondering what happened to me."

Still no answer.

"Poppa might be awake."

"Stop making excuses," he said. "If you're going to leave, then leave."

"I don't want to," she said. She turned in his arms, leaning on his chest and presented her mouth to him. He captured it, and for a few long, sweet moments there were no more words.

"But I have to go," she said, after the kiss, and he opened his arms to allow her out.

He watched as she got dressed. He had always enjoyed watching women dress, but never like this. He devoured every move that she made, at the same time hating every move, because the closer she came to being dressed, the closer she came to leaving—and he didn't want her to leave.

Ever.

"This is very scary," he said to her.

She stopped, looked at him, and said, "Yes, it is very scary, but it's also very right. You must feel it too."

"I do," he told her. "I feel it—and that's what scares the hell out of me."

She approached the bed and put her hand on his shoulder.

"I'm not asking for any promises, Clint," she said. "You know that."

"I know."

"I want you to know though that whatever happens between us is up to you."

He put his hand over hers, lifted it off his shoulder, and kissed it tenderly.

"I know."

She leaned over, brushed her hair out of the way, and kissed him warmly.

"Good night," she said. "I'll see you in the morning."

"Good night," he said.

He watched her leave, then lay back on the bed with his hands clasped behind his head and stared at the ceiling. He couldn't deny it any longer, even though they'd only known each other one day.

It was right.

Now what was he going to do about it?

THIRTY-EIGHT

Clint awoke the next morning feeling refreshed. Joanna Morgan was on his mind and he felt good, even happy, but then the rest of it came back and his mood changed.

He got up and washed with the water in the basin by the window. While he was drying there was a knock on the door. He knew it wasn't Joanna, because it was a man's knock, so he assumed it was Estle.

"Good morning," Clint said, backing away so the gambler could enter.

"Not judging from the look on your face," Estle said, shutting the door. "What happened to you yesterday?"

"What do you mean?"

"What do I mean?" Estle asked. "You did a disappearing act after you showed me that telegram."

"I was around," Clint said, throwing down the towel and picking up his shirt.

"Would you like to let me in on what's going on?"

"What do you mean?"

"Are you being deliberately dense today?"

Clint paused, then said, "I don't know, maybe I am."

"Would you like to explain that to me?"

"Yeah, I guess you deserve an explanation," Clint said, and gave him one.

Estle listened patiently as Clint explained everything he

had learned since his visit with the sheriff of Northway.

"Mallerby was a phony?" he said, afterward.

"That's the way it looks."

"Where's the military commander stationed?" the gambler asked.

"Anchorage, I think."

"Seems to me your next step would be to send a telegram there and find out if he even has an assistant, find out why somebody from his office wasn't in Cordova to greet you."

"Yeah, I guess that would be a smart move," Clint said, buttoning his shirt.

"Say, what's the matter with you, anyway?" Estle demanded, frowning at Clint. "You ain't in love, are you?"

"What makes you ask that?" Clint asked, cautiously.

"I've seen men act like you're acting when they're in love," Estle said.

"Is this the way you acted in Wyoming?"

Estle made a face and said, "Don't bring that up, please."

Clint strapped on his gun and said, "Now that you know you're not wanted by the law, what are your plans?"

"I don't know," Estle said. "I sort of thought I'd tag along with you until the end. Now it looks to me like you want to quit right here."

"What else can I do?"

"Try and find him," Estle said. "Send some telegrams to the surrounding towns. Make an effort."

"Go through the motions, you mean."

"If that's the way you want to look at it," Estle said. "I assume you're getting paid for this job."

"I'm not a bounty hunter," Clint snapped.

"I didn't say you were," Estle said. "Look, maybe I'm wasting my time."

"Maybe you are," Clint agreed. "You're not wanted by the law, so you're free to go home, if you want."

"I guess I'd better," the gambler said. Shaking his head, he left the room.

Clint almost called out to Estle before he left, but a moment's hesitation and it was too late. It was just as well, anyway. If he did decide to abandon the search for Martel, and stay here with Joanna, he didn't need Estle around as a constant reminder.

Suddenly, he was stunned. That had been the first time he had consciously thought of giving it all up for Joanna, a woman he'd known for only one day.

He rubbed both hands over his face, then picked up his hat and left the room. Before he made the final decision, maybe he was better off sending a couple of more telegrams.

THIRTY-NINE

Clint had the telegram drafted in his mind by the time he reached the office, so he recited it to the boy, and told him to send the same telegraph to Glenallen, Teton, Tenacross, and two or three other towns surrounding Northway.

"When you get the answers, I'll most likely—"

"—be in the saloon?" the boy asked.

"Try the hotel first," Clint said, tossed him two bits, and left.

Clint had sent the telegrams on the assumption that Martel would have headed for Canada, and not gone farther north in Alaska. If that didn't pan out, he'd give it up and decide what he was going to do about Joanna. One thing he knew for sure, he didn't want her to go out of his life, but beyond that . . .

When he had come downstairs to the lobby, Morgan had been behind the counter.

"Guess I pooped out on you, huh, boy?" the old man asked.

"We both fell asleep, Morgan," Clint said. "No harm done."

"Going out for breakfast?"

"After a stop, yes," Clint said.

"Joanna is still asleep," he said. "She must have had a late night, huh?"

"Now, Morgan," Clint said, mustering what was left of

his good humor that morning, "how would I know anything about that?"

He left the old man cackling behind the desk, and made his way to the telegraph office.

Once the telegrams were sent, he went to the restaurant for breakfast. When Lisa brought the coffee she asked, "Are you gonna be staying in Northway, Mr. Adams?"

"Clint," he corrected her, "and I don't rightly know at the moment, Lisa. Why?"

"Well, me and my folks was talking, about how happy Joanna looked yesterday." The girl lowered her head shyly, then blurted out, "We think it's because of you."

"Is that a fact?"

"Joanna's real nice, Clint," Lisa said. "I hope you decide to stay on."

"Well, thank you, Lisa," Clint said. "I'll make sure that when I decide, you'll be one of the first to know."

"Golly," the girl said and went to get his breakfast.

While he ate breakfast, he marveled at how other people had been able to see what was going on between himself and Joanna. Was it that obvious? After fighting it for so long, should he let his guard down and allow himself to feel, totally, for Joanna Morgan?

He left his breakfast half uneaten, but finished the pot of coffee and ordered another.

"Anything wrong with the breakfast?" Lisa asked, looking gravely concerned.

"No, Lisa, nothing's wrong with the food," he assured her.

"Are you feeling all right?"

Clint smiled at the girl and said, "Yes, Mother, I'm feeling just fine. I just wasn't as hungry as I thought."

Relief showed on Lisa's pretty, chubby face, and she turned to serve other customers.

Clint finished off the second pot of coffee, and was at a loss for what to do next—except go to Joanna. In point of fact, that was all he wanted to do—and since he had to wait for replies to his last few telegrams before doing anything else anyway, he might just as well spend the time with her.

As Clint left the small café, he was so intent on seeing Joanna that he didn't see L.D. Estle watching him, didn't notice that the gambler was on his tail as he made his way down the street to the hotel.

Things had been going along just as planned, Estle thought, as he followed the Gunsmith, and now all of a sudden, they were going wrong. Still, it was encouraging that Clint had sent out those telegrams, and Estle had to admit that Joanna Morgan was a beautiful woman. Maybe the Gunsmith still had time to snap out of it and get the job done.

Estle hoped so. He hated the idea of having to start from step one, all over again.

And he knew damn well that Fenton would hate it even more than he did.

Neither Clint, nor Estle, saw the man who was watching the Gunsmith from a rooftop across the street. Clint was too intent on Joanna, and Estle was too intent on Clint.

The only thing Paul Martel was intent on was killing the Gunsmith.

FORTY

When Clint entered the hotel, Morgan looked up from behind the desk.

"Back already?"

"Couldn't stay away."

The old man cackled and said, "I know it wasn't 'cause you couldn't wait to see me again."

"Oh, you know that, do you?"

Morgan cackled again and said, "She's in the back, slaving over those damned books again. Son, I'll tell you a secret," the old man said, leaning on the desk.

Clint came closer and said, "What's that?"

"She ain't never gonna get those books to balance, no matter how hard she tries."

"Maybe she won't have to try much longer," Clint said.

"Damn, son," Morgan said, "I was hopin' you'd say that."

Estle stopped outside the hotel and took a quick look inside. Clint was going through a curtained doorway behind the desk, and a balding, toothless old man was cackling away like crazy. Since he also had a room in the hotel, he knew that the old man was the owner, Joanna Morgan's father. He had to guess that Joanna was behind that curtain.

He crossed the street and stepped into a doorway from

where he could see the front of the hotel, but someone coming out of the hotel would not be able to readily spot him.

He folded his arms and settled down to wait.

Above Estle, on the roof of the very same building, Paul Martel settled down with his Winchester '73, also to wait.

The pain Martel had felt when Clint Adams put down the uprising of his New South had not dimmed over the years. In fact it had grown like a fire, fanned by his desire for revenge against the man who had done nothing but put him behind schedule. The fool had let him go, thinking that he was finished, and that was what would be his undoing.

Martel's plan—after the botched assassination attempt on the President—had been to cross Alaska into Canada, and then back into the United States. However, when he had gotten the telegram from his man in Cordova, that the man they had sent after him was none other than the Gunsmith, his plans changed.

A chance—finally a chance to take his vengeance on Clint Adams. Adams was smart, and using the mountains to bypass Glenallen was something he would do. Martel decided that all he had to do was stay out of sight while in Northway, and wait.

A lot of waiting, but it had paid off. Clint Adams had walked right into his arms.

His initial plan for Adams had been to let him know who was killing him, but he quickly changed that. The Gunsmith was too dangerous a foe to play games with. The next time he walked out of the hotel, he was a dead man, and that was all that mattered.

"Struggling with the books again?" Clint asked Joanna.

She looked up from the desk, swept her hair out of her eyes and said, "Still."

"What would you say if I told you to forget them?"

She bit her lower lip and said, "I'd say, are you sure?"

"No," he admitted, "I'm not."

"It was only one day," she reminded him.

"That's not it, Joanna," he said. "I'm sure about you, I'm just not sure about me."

"Well, I'm sure about both of us," she said, standing up and walking up to him, "and I'm sure enough for both of us. Incredible as it seems, I love you." She slid her arms around his neck and pulled him down so she could kiss him. "And I think you love me."

"Joanna—"

She touched her index finger to his lips, and shook her head.

"Don't say it now, Clint," she told him, "say it when you're sure, and you mean it."

He put his arms around her waist and held her lightly.

"I sent some telegrams today," he said. "I've got to go and pick up the answers. If they're the right answers—for us—then I'll come back, and I'll tell you, so that you can't doubt that it's what I feel."

She squeezed his waist and said, "I'll walk you out."

When they came out from behind the curtain with their arms around each other's waist, old Morgan began to cackle again.

"I knew it, I knew it!"

"Oh, stop cackling like an old hen, Poppa," she scolded her father. "Nothing's been settled."

"It will be," he said, "it will be, and that's the bitchin' truth!"

"Ignore him," she told Clint, and they walked together to the front door.

To Estle, it all seemed to happen in slow motion, which is the way it always seemed when you were helpless.

Clint and Joanna came out the door, arms around each

other. As they stepped out the door, Joanna swung around in front of Clint, probably to give him a kiss, and that was when Estle heard the shot.

He watched as the bullet entered Joanna's back, and she stiffened in Clint's arms. As he lowered her to the ground, he saw the second bullet strike Clint in the left shoulder, spinning him backward.

Joanna had not made a sound when the bullet struck her, but when Clint was hit, she cried out something that might have been his name.

Estle finally moved then, vaulting out of the doorway, but he was too late. . . .

The first shot was well placed, Martel thought. If the girl hadn't swung around in front of Adams, it would all have been over. The second shot was rushed, which was why it had struck high, and to the left. There was no time for a third shot.

That would have to come later.

"I couldn't catch him," Estle told Clint later. "He moved too fast. I couldn't tell which way he went."

Clint sat stiffly on the bed in his room while the doctor bandaged his shoulder, having already removed the bullet and cleaned the wound.

"I've told you what he looks like—was it him?" he asked.

"Yes. I saw his face clearly, just for a split second," Estle said, "but it was Martel."

Clint closed his eyes and silently cursed himself.

"There was nothing you could have done, Clint," Estle hastened to say. "There was nothing anyone could have done."

"I could have found him," Clint said, "and stopped him. If I had, Joanna would still be alive now."

The doctor finished his work and told Clint, "You'll have to restrict your movements for a while, until it heals properly."

"I don't have time for that," Clint said, standing up and struggling into a clean shirt.

"If you open that wound again—" the doctor started, but Estle stopped him, paid him, and sent him on his way.

"Clint," he said, turning towards the Gunsmith, "I know you're in a lot of pain at the moment, and I don't only mean your shoulder, but you've got to stop and think—"

"About what?" the Gunsmith asked, strapping on his gun and wincing at the pain it caused.

"About yourself," Estle said. "If that wound opens, you could get it infected—"

"I don't care about that."

"Well, you should."

"I've got to catch him, L.D." Clint said. "This time I've got to stop him for good."

Estle paused helplessly, then said, "I think we'd better get a drink and talk about some things. I know you could use a drink."

Clint looked at the gambler, and said, "All right, but I am going after him, with you or without you."

"We'll talk about it," Estle said.

Downstairs Mrs. Evans was behind the desk, dabbing at her tear-filled eyes with a lace hankie.

"How is he, Mrs. Evans?" Clint asked, approaching the desk.

"He's in the back," she said. "He just sits there, staring, not speaking. Perhaps you should speak to him."

"I will," he said, "but not right now."

Not while he was feeling so guilty, he added to himself. After he caught Martel, then he'd be able to talk to Morgan.

As they left the hotel Estle said, "You can't place all the guilt on your own shoulders like this, Clint."

"Oh, I'm not taking all of the guilt, L.D.," the Gunsmith said. "A good portion of it, yes, but I'm saving some for Paul Martel." In a remarkably calm, cold voice he said, "I'm saving a good portion of it for Mr. Martel."

FORTY-ONE

They sat at a back table in the saloon with a bottle of whiskey. When Clint threw down his first drink and poured a second, Estle said, "You better take it easy on that stuff, Clint. That won't solve anything."

"Don't worry," Clint said. "I won't get drunk." To himself he added, *I'll just drink enough to make the pain in my shoulder bearable.*

"Tell me about yourself, L.D.," Clint said. "Who are you, really?"

"You know my name," Estle said, "what you don't know is that I was sent in to back you up."

"Fenton?"

Estle nodded.

"He did it to me again, didn't he?"

"I don't know what you—"

"That bastard! He sent me in knowing that when Martel found out it was me on his trail he'd stop and wait for me. It was the best chance he had of getting him."

"You just said it," Estle said. "It was Fenton's best chance, and he took it. You can't fault him for that."

"Sure I can," Clint said. "I'm tired of being a puppet on that man's string. Twice he's done it, and that's two times too many."

"We're all puppets, Clint."

"Yeah, but you are by choice," Clint said. "I'm finished being tricked into doing his work for him."

"All right," Estle said, "let's put that aside for now. Where would Martel go now?"

"And where has he been hiding out this whole time?" Clint added. "Somebody in this town has been giving him a place to stay."

"He tried for you and missed, though," Estle said. "What will he do now?"

"He'll run," Clint said. "He'll try and find another place to hole up and wait for me." Clint leaned forward, and Estle could see the rage behind his eyes. "I've got to catch up to him before then."

"We'll need Chooka for that," Estle said.

"Is he still in town?"

"He's around."

"I can't figure him out," Clint said. "The phony Mallerby sent him to us, but he never did anything but guide us."

"If Martel figured you for going through the mountains, maybe he just wanted to make sure you made it. He had his man get you a good guide."

"Maybe," Clint said. "Find him, L.D. Let's hear what he's got to say for himself."

"I'll find him," Estle said. "Believe it or not, Clint, I want to help you."

"Then do it," Clint said. "Find Chooka."

"You got it."

Estle got up and left and Clint put the cork back in the bottle. It would have been very easy to sit there and finish the bottle and try and drown everything out, but Estle had been right. That wouldn't solve anything. The only thing that would do that was catching Paul Martel.

And even that wouldn't bring Joanna back.

He signaled the bartender to bring him a beer, and settled

down to wait for Estle, with only the dull pain in his shoulder for company.

It was barely a half an hour later when Estle walked in with Chooka.

"Hey," the bartender yelled right away, "no Indians in here."

Clint looked over at the man and said, "You want to try putting him out?"

The bartender saw the look in the Gunsmith's eyes, and quickly found a glass that needed cleaning.

"Sit down, Chooka," Clint said.

The Indian sat and regarded Clint stolidly.

"Have you heard what happened?"

"I have heard," he said. "I am sorry your woman was killed."

"Yeah," Clint said. "Chooka, I have to know why you came with us from Cordova."

The Indian shrugged and said, "To guide you."

"Nothing more?"

"I do not lie," Chooka said.

Clint studied the man's face, and then said, "No, I don't suppose that you do."

"You're going to believe him?" Estle asked.

"I don't have a choice," Clint said.

"He could be lying."

"You've been working for Fenton for too long," Clint said. "Look at this man's eyes. He's not lying." Clint turned to Chooka and said, "We want to take the fastest route to the border, Chooka. Do you know of such a route?"

"Of course. When do you want to leave?"

"Now," Clint said, standing up.

"You are wounded."

"I want to leave now." Clint turned to Estle. "Are you coming?"

Estle nodded and said, "If only to keep you on your horse."

"Let's go, then," Clint said. He took out some money and gave it to Chooka. "Get some supplies, and we'll meet you at the livery stable."

The Indian took the money, nodded, and left, drawing his chilkat close around him.

"You're not going to be able to take the cold, Clint," Estle said. "You look feverish now."

"I'm fine," Clint lied. "L.D., check with the livery. Martel had to keep his horse somewhere."

"All right. I'll meet you over there."

Estle started to get up, but stopped halfway and stuck his hand in his pocket.

"I almost forgot," he said.

"What?"

He handed Clint a handful of yellow telegraph messages, and said, "None of the other towns remember seeing anyone matching Martel's description—"

"That doesn't mean anything anymore," Clint said.

"—but you might be interested in the telegram from the office of the military commander."

Clint held Estle's eyes and said, "You tell me."

"They had sent a man to meet you at Cordova, but he was killed. They found his body on the trail."

"Is that all?"

"No. They caught the man who was using the name John Mallerby," Estle said. "He was part of Martel's New South movement."

"He didn't talk like any southerner I ever met," Clint said.

"Well, the fact that he was being paid well made up for his not having been from the south. Seems he was some kind of mercenary, working for the highest bidder. If the Indians paid him, he'd swear he was part Indian."

Clint left the telegrams on the table top and stood up.

"So there's only Martel," Clint said.

"Once we get him, the New South will be dead for good," Estle said, "just like the old one."

"Let's get moving, then," Clint said. "The sooner that happens, the better off we'll all be."

Clint left the saloon with Estle, and walked to the hotel. He didn't stop in the lobby until he had collected his saddlebags and rifle and was on his way out.

"Is he still in there?" he asked Mrs. Evans.

"Yes," she said. "He hasn't moved."

He stared at the curtained doorway, but he didn't have the courage to go in. Maybe later . . .

As he turned to leave Mrs. Evans asked, "Will you be back, Mr. Adams?"

"I hope so, Mrs. Evans," he said. "I've got a lot of explaining to do to that man in there. I only hope he'll be able to find it in his heart to forgive me."

The woman looked puzzled, but the Gunsmith offered no explanation. If Martel had started out immediately, there wasn't a moment to lose.

FORTY-TWO

Outside of Northway, they stopped while Chooka checked for sign.

"We've got to hope that he goes for the border in a straight line," Estle said.

"He will," Clint said, staring towards the border, as if he could see Martel.

When they had met at the livery, Estle had some good news for Clint. The livery man had known of another place someone could have put their horse up, and Estle found out that a man fitting Martel's description had kept a horse there for nearly a week.

Chooka got up from his knee now and returned to his horse. He mounted up and looked at Clint.

"A horse and rider passed here maybe two hours ago, maybe more."

"Has to be him," Clint said.

"Nobody else took a horse out of the livery," Estle said, "or from the other fella's barn. He didn't see Martel take his horse, but when I asked him to go out and check, that was the only animal missing."

"It's him," Clint said again. "It's got to be."

"He is going in a straight line," Chooka said, pointing. Then he pointed east and said, "We go this way."

Chooka had explained that between Northway and the

177

border was a gorge. You would either have to go around it, or pick your way across it, but either way it would take time. He was taking them around the gorge as of now, and Martel wouldn't find out about it until he got there.

"Can we beat him to the border?" Clint asked. "Or will we just close the ground between us?"

Chooka said, "I think we will beat him there . . . but we will have to wait and see."

Chooka took the lead and Clint and Estle fell in behind him.

"We'll beat him or close ground," Estle said, "if he doesn't know this country, and doesn't know about the gorge."

"You're back to your cheerful self, I see," Clint said.

"Clint—"

"You can turn back anytime, L.D."

"I'll stick it out," Estle said.

"Quietly," Clint said, and Estle didn't answer.

Go in a straight line, Clint mentally screamed at Martel. *Please!*

"Clint!" Estle said, and Clint felt his right arm being jogged.

"Huh?"

"You're dozing off in the saddle," Estle said. "Are you all right?"

"Fine," he lied.

Actually, he was sweating inside his coat, and knew that he had a fever, but he had no intention of going back now. Not without Martel.

"Chooka," he called.

The Indian stopped and turned around.

"Can we pick up the pace?"

"There is no need," Chooka said. "We are making good time."

"Pick up the pace, anyway," Clint said. "I want to make sure we get there first."

"You're not going to be able to take it," Estle said.

"Shut up!"

When Martel reached the rocky gorge he cursed aloud. He had not wanted to hire a guide and preferred to rely on the map he had bought as part of his plan to assassinate the President. Alaska was his choice all along for a place to hide out, whether or not he was successful. He had purchased the map with that in mind, but the goddamned map did not show this gorge. It was the first time the map had failed him, but it was a critical time.

Now he had to decide whether to go around or through the gorge. Once he was on the other side, he might find the Gunsmith waiting for him. He did not expect Adams's wound to slow him down, not after what had happened to the woman.

According to the map, there were two ideal points at which to cross the border into Alaska. He and Adams had a fifty-fifty chance of picking the same point. Martel was convinced that it would be better if they did, rather than have them miss each other. The famous Gunsmith was wounded, and ready to be taken.

Martel made his decision and urged his pony down into the gorge.

Be on the other side, Adams, Martel thought, *but if you're not, don't worry.*

I'll wait for you.

As it turned out, the increased pace was more of a help to

the Gunsmith than a hindrance. It kept him awake and reasonably alert. Thinking about Martel did the rest.

Chooka lifted his right hand in a signal to stop, and Clint rode up next to him.

Chooka pointed and said, "The border."

To Clint the land looked no different, but the Indian knew what he was talking about.

"Where will he cross, Chooka?" he asked.

The Indian shrugged and said, "There are many places, but perhaps two are best."

"Then we'll have to split up," Clint said, looking at Estle. "You take one, and we'll take the other."

"Are you sure—"

"I'll keep Chooka with me," Clint said, heading off Estle's objections.

They rode along until Chooka once again called for them to stop.

"If he crosses here he will be able to go onto Fort Selkirk," the Indian said. "Further up is a crossing that would lead him to the town of Dawson."

"No other towns?" Clint asked.

"Not close to the border," the Indian said.

"All right," Clint said. He turned to Estle and said, "You stay here, we'll ride further on."

"If he comes my way," Estle said, "I'm not saving him for you, Clint. I'm going to do my job."

"I thought your job was to back me up."

"Or take care of Martel," Estle added, "whichever presented itself."

Clint thought it over a moment, then said, "It doesn't matter. He'll come to me."

"There's a fifty-fifty chance he'll go either way," Estle pointed out.

Clint shook his head stubbornly and said, "He'll be drawn to me, L.D. You'll see."

"Well, I wish you luck," Estle said.

"Let's go, Chooka," Clint said.

It was almost an hour's ride before Chooka stopped.

"Here," he said.

Clint looked around. There was a cluster of rock formations that afforded good shelter from the cold, and would also hide them from sight.

"We'll put the horses behind there, Chooka," Clint said, "and you stay with them."

"You will be able to approach this man alone?" Chooka asked. His voice reflected no particular concern, simply a need to know.

"I'll handle him alone," Clint said. "If he gets past me, you have no obligation to try and stop him."

The Indian nodded, and they made for the rocks.

Clint dismounted and allowed Chooka to take Duke's reins, making sure that the big black would go with him. The Indian took the horses to where they would have the best shelter, and then returned to Clint's side. He did not say anything, but simply pulled his chilkat closer around him.

Later, he said, "He will come from there," and pointed. "You will see him, but he will not be close. You will have to wait."

"I'll wait," Clint said, through clenched teeth. "I'll wait until hell freezes over, if I have to."

It didn't take that long.

"He comes," Chooka said. When he noticed that the Gunsmith had dozed off and not heard, he nudged him slightly and said again, louder, "He comes."

"I wasn't asleep," Clint said thickly, rubbing his eyes. "Where?"

"There," the Indian said, pointing.

Clint tried to push himself away from the rocks, but had to

make two attempts before he was able to stand steadily on his feet.

He clenched and unclenched his gunhand and thought, *Don't fail me now*. He tried to clench his left hand, but it wouldn't close. It struck him fleetingly that he could not feel anything in that arm, but he would worry about that later.

As he watched Martel approach, he was able to make out the man's handsome features.

Clint remembered him as a tall, well-built, handsome man in his early forties. That was in New Orleans. Out here in the cold of the Alaskan plains, this version looked older, thinner, a different Paul Martel.

Martel stopped about twenty yards away from the rock formation, and Clint knew that Martel could feel his presence. He stepped away from the rocks, out into the open, propelled by unsteady legs.

Martel smiled, and he hated him for it. He had no right to smile like that.

He had no right to live.

FORTY-THREE

Martel urged his horse forward, closed the distance by half, and then stopped.

"You look terrible, Clint," he called out.

The Gunsmith didn't answer.

"I know I hit you—where was it, on the left shoulder? Must hurt like hell, huh?"

No answer.

"I've been waiting for this for a long time," Martel went on. "I was a fair hand with a gun when you last saw me, did you know that? Never got a chance to show you, and now I'm even better. Maybe that wound in your shoulder evens things up, eh?"

Clint didn't answer. He kept his eyes on Martel, who was wearing a blanket as a poncho. He remembered that the man was right-handed, and he watched Martel's right shoulder.

"I'm going to throw back this blanket, Clint, so my gun will be free, and then we'll see. Okay? I won't even dismount, because when I'm done I'll ride right past your body, pausing only to spit on it. And then I'll go back and take care of General Grant. The New South will rise yet, Clint, as soon as I get rid of its two worst enemies. You and Grant."

Stop talking, Clint thought. *Make your move before I pass out.*

The figure of Martel astride his horse began to waver as fever distorted his vision, but he kept his eyes pinned to the man's right shoulder.

"I'm thowing back this blanket, now, and—"

The rest of Martel's words were never spoken, for as the Gunsmith saw his shoulder tense, and dip slightly, he drew his gun in one swift, effortless motion, and fired.

As the bullet struck Martel in the chest, the gun that had been in his hand the whole time discharged, punching and burning its way through the blanket as it flew harmlessly through the air. Martel tumbled off his horse backward, his legs flipping over his head, and crashed to the dirt with bone-jarring force.

Keeping his gun out, Clint closed the ground between them, planting his feet with care for fear that they would go out from under him. At one point, Martel's horse pranced in his direction, and he barely sidestepped the frightened animal in time, staggering as he did so. Finally, he reached the fallen man, who was still alive.

"Christ," Martel said. He was lying on his back, breathing heavily. "Christ," he said again. "It hurts."

"Good," Clint said, speaking for the first time.

Martel's eyes sought the Gunsmith's face and held his enemy's eyes steadily, despite the pain.

"Damn you, Adams," he said. "You finally killed my dream, didn't you?" Martel began to cough, and blood gushed from his mouth to cover his chest. He turned his head to the side, hawked and spat, and then looked back at Clint Adams.

"You killed my dream, but I think maybe when that woman took your bullet, I killed yours too, huh?"

He laughed, and once again blood flowed from his mouth. He spat again and said, "Maybe that thought will keep me happy in hell, eh?"

He was still laughing, with blood pouring from his mouth, when Clint Adams shot him between the eyes.

FORTY-FOUR

It was decided that they would take the body back to Northway with them. There Clint would talk to Morgan while Estle sent a telegram to Fenton in San Francisco.

"You want me to say anything for you?" Estle asked Clint in front of the hotel.

Clint dismounted and stared up at Estle, then said, "Tell him—tell him I'm coming back to San Francisco, and I'd advise that he not be there when I arrive."

Estle held the reins of Martel's horse, with the dead man tied to the saddle, and started for the undertaker's office with it. Chooka left them there, and neither man would ever see him again.

Clint walked into the hotel and found Mrs. Evans behind the desk, apparently cleaning it out.

"Mrs. Evans?" he called.

She looked up at him, and the tears sprung anew from her eyes.

"Oh, Mr. Adams," she said.

"What happened?" he asked, approaching the desk. "Where's Morgan."

"He just . . . went," she said, shrugging her shoulders. "He was sitting in his chair, and he just . . . up and died. The doctor said he had no reason to live anymore."

"He's dead?" Clint said.

She nodded and dabbed at her eyes with her lace hankie.

"When?"

"Right after you left."

They had been forced to camp overnight before starting back with Martel's body, so Morgan had died the day before.

"I'm sorry," Mrs. Evans said.

"I'm sorry too, Mrs. Evans," he said, "but I don't even have anyone to say it to."

He turned and walked out into the street.

Estle found Clint in the saloon, sitting over a glass of whiskey.

"Did you see the old man?"

"No," Clint said, "but you might have."

"What do you mean?"

"At the undertaker's," Clint said. "Morgan died yesterday, right after we left."

"Oh," Estle said. He went to the bar and came back with a glass of whiskey of his own. "I'm sorry," he said, sitting across from Clint.

"I didn't have a chance to explain, L.D.," Clint said.

"He didn't blame you, Clint," Estle said. "I'm sure of that."

"I wish I could be."

They both drank their whiskey in a silent toast, and set the glasses down.

"Some good should come out of this," Clint finally said.

Estle looked at him and said, "How? We did what we came to Alaska to do, but if you ask me, the price was too high."

"Then let's lower it a little," Clint said.

"How?" Estle asked again.

"Do you still want to go back to Cordova?"

"Wilma Sue?" Estle asked, after a moment.

Clint nodded.

"Wilma Sue," he said.